JUKE

T.K. RICHARDS

To the girls that fall fast.

Be careful not to let it cloud your judgment.
One is never safe when one is in love.

The Serpent Queen

Note From The Author

PLEASE NOTE THIS BOOK CONTAINS WORDS AND DIALECT FROM CERTAIN CHARACTERS THAT **DO NOT REFLECT** TRADITIONAL ENGLISH. SOME WORDS ARE CHOPPED AND/OR SPELLED TO REFLECT HOW THE CHARACTERS SPEAK.

FOR EXAMPLE

INNIT is a regional word short for AREN'T I RIGHT? And also short for AIN'T IT.
YOU may sometimes reflect YOU HAVE.
'BOUT will be short for ABOUT.

Thanks for recognizing varied southern accents in this work.

Introduction

There are love stories where two people meet by chance. They fall in love and capture something special people would die to experience...Loving each other until the end of time. For us, the end was never clear, but the song of our time together is a story where passion meets destiny, and love connects two kindred souls. This is our ballad.

Chapter 1
Give It Up

In less than five seconds, I knew I was going to fuck Cade Williamson. The moment his honey eyes glazed over me, and the sun kissed his ripped biceps while the chords in his hands squeezed the leather handles on his motorcycle, I was his.

He looked at me with a grin on the side of his lips, then blew me a kiss. "You riding with me?"

Giddy with adventurous eyes and hot in the ass, I mouthed. "Yeah."

The whiteness of his teeth, and the seductive, sexy grin on his full lips made my yoni pulse on its own. Just looking at him lubed my thighs as he captivated me. Casting some sort of spell my defenses didn't try to fight.

I threw away all of the rules from the handbook of one night stands, and found a version of myself that had been waiting to blossom. The risk taker, buried deep within the dark corners of my inhibitions. The foolish girl infatuated with love rose to the forefront, and burned my morals to dust.

He sank the top row of his teeth into his bottom lip and called me over with his eyes.

"Turn around," he said with authority.

"Why?"

"Can't ride you 'round if you're wearing a thong. Five-O is throwing bikers in jail for that down here."

I threw my crossbody bag behind me. "I'm not wearing a thong. You'll have to find another crafty way to check out my ass." I placed my hand on his shoulder and hopped on the back of his motorcycle.

"Challenge accepted."

His friend pointed to Kandi and DeVaughn. The duo I traveled with to Myrtle Beach. A duo unworthy of being called my friends.

"Tell your girls to come, too," the friend said.

"Shit, you ain't gotta ask me twice." Kandi hurdled onto his bike.

Devaughn followed suit and jumped on one of the other bikes in the motorcade. We merged into traffic and our drivers sped down the road. Suddenly the bike jerked and I squeezed my driver's stomach too tight.

"Oh shit." I gasped, as deep breaths and squeals expelled from my lips.

Cade looked back at me. "You alright?"

"Yeah." I lied, readjusting my hands around his waist.

He reached back and rubbed my thigh. "I got you."

My southern slit did a kegel while I buried my face on his back as a light commotion amongst the drivers on the road turned confrontational when we stopped.

"We see y'all," said one of Cade's friends.

A male voice yelled back over the revving motors. "I don't mean no disrespect, fellas, but that was dangerous how you pulled out! You have ladies on your bikes! Be gentlemen and be safe out here!"

"We will. You go ahead." Kandi's driver shouted back.

She and I faced each other with stretched eyes.

"Is that the guy from *The Cosby Show*?" she asked.

The man turned around and smiled.

"Oh shit, that is him." I laughed out loud as the actor sped off with his crew.

The six of us drove up the strip at high speed once in the clear. I held onto my speed demon switching gears wanting him to catch up to Robert from *The Cosby Show,* in disbelief he spoke up on our behalf, and thinking about what he'd said.

I'd put my safety in jeopardy for an easy, cheap thrill. My spirit chastised me for breaking my vow to never get on one of those things, yet there I was on the dark, crowded beach streets packed with motorcycle clubs and horny men, spreading my legs open for a ride.

It was reckless and stupid. Me in a blue two piece bathing suit, helmet-less, putting my life in danger at the hands of a stranger. I could have skinned my flawless golden legs, or died squeezing the tight chest of a man whose name I didn't know.

The thrill suddenly left me. Fear filled my veins and my hands began to suffocate Cade.

"You hungry?" He smiled back at me.

"I could go for a bite."

He signaled for his crew to pull over on the main street. They parked in five car spaces on the lot at a local wing house. Cade lowered the kick stand with his foot and climbed off the bike.

He faced me. "Watch out for that pipe. I wouldn't want you to burn those pretty stems."

My cheeks burst until they were red as he inched closer. "Thanks for telling me. I have no idea what I'm doing on this thing."

"I can tell."

"How so?"

"You were squeezing me hella tight. That's why I pulled over to see if you were alright."

"Thanks for looking out for me."

"It's cool. I won't let anything happen to you." He drew a J on the middle of my thigh with his knuckles. "I told you. I got you."

"I don't even know your name, but I'm supposed to believe you *"got"* me."

"It's Cade. But people call me Juke. I already know yours."

"How is that?"

"Your friend called you J.C. when I pulled up."

'Hmm. Cute and observant.'

I smiled to myself. "It's Jaya. Jaya Marcel."

He scowled. "What's the C stand for?"

"Chanelle."

"Jaya Chanelle Marcel. Is your mother a poet?"

I glared at him.

"I'm just kidding around, Jaya Chanelle. Others can call you J.C. I'm gonna call you Sweetness." He pursed his lips. "Where are you from, Sweetness?"

"Fayetteville."

"I didn't know they make'm like you in Fayettenam."

"I hear that all the time. Don't know what you all mean by that...But, whatever. And you?"

"Virginia, but born and raised in West Virginia."

"Humph. I didn't think black people lived in West Virginia until my favorite player, Randy Moss got drafted."

He laughed. "Pretty and a footballer." He shouted to Kandi's driver. "Mike! She loves Moss!"

"You got you a smart one!" Mike clicked his teeth.

Cade smiled at me. "What you know about football?"

"I'm from the south. I know everything about it. Call me when the season starts. I'll help you with the spread."

"Well damn." He pinched my chin. "What do you do?"

"I work at a hotel part-time, and go to school, but my passion is music."

"You sing?"

"I compose. Write lyrics and sing background in a local band. Waiting for the day we blow up. What do you do?"

"Ironically I play football. I ain't Moss or nothing, but I do pretty good, and run my own comm company."

"Just say you don't want to tell me."

"I'm serious. I'm on the practice team for The Skins."

"What's that like?"

"It's alright. Not what I dreamed I would be doing, but it's a pretty good living."

"And what's a comm company?"

"Communications. I sell new tech equipment as it's developed to upgrade company systems."

"Sounds complicated."

"It can be if you're not into tech."

"I'm not. I still miss having a flip phone."

He laughed at me as if I was joking, but I was serious. My eyes shifted to the beads of stubble on his chest above the button on his shirt. His brown skin looked like it tasted of sweet brown sugar and agave. Naughty thoughts owned my mind as we conversed a short round of "Tell me about yourself" and shared a tray of wings and fries before hitting the open road.

My concern with safety and living recklessly fell to the back of my mind once we were reacquainted into close quarters, and intimacy rebuilt between us as I held onto him. The man brought out the closeted slut in me. The inexperienced little girl who was ready to try new things, and finally know what it meant to "pop that pussy."

For most of my brief adult life, I was a relationship kind of girl. Fresh out of a one year relationship with a liar, and before him a three year relationship with my high school sweetheart. I hadn't a clue about seduction, mouth suction, or free fucking, and the eagerness to learn what I was missing in the streets could no longer be contained when I stared into Cade's mysterious eyes flashing back at me.

The feel of his body in my arms and the smell of his watery cologne aroused me in ways I didn't know existed. As Blanche Devereaux would say, "He brought out the artist in me." The singer looking to sing into his microphone.

I yearned to do forbidden things with this man. Things that had never crossed my mind before. Acts I labeled as whorish and improper when my band mates spoke of their wild weekends with loose women. Cade brought out such desire in me to become one of those tawdry women with him. And I decided not to fight the urges blossoming in my garden.

Our bodies were glued together from the moisture in the night air, and strong gusts propelling from the shore. For hours, the wind blew my hair out of my face as I pressed it in the center of his back, listening to his heart thump in my ear. My clasped hands unraveled against his chest, copping a feel of the steel pecs below his furlow.

He felt the back of my hand. "You're cold?"

I shivered as he pulled over to the side of the road.

"Here you go." He unbuttoned his shirt and wrapped it around me.

I slipped my arms through the sleeves. "Thank you."

He bestowed an endearing smile. "Are you here for the whole weekend?"

"We're leaving five o'clock Sunday morning."

He exhaled. "I thought you were about to say five o'clock in the morning."

I smiled at him. "What if I had?"

"I wouldn't let you," he teased. "Hold on. Let's catch up with the others."

It was a mystery why I felt safe with Cade hot tailing it in the dark streets, and swerving in and out of cars. But as he instructed, I held on, loving every minute my body was clung to his.

DeVaughn and her driver turned in early, while Kandi and I continued to enjoy our midnight madness. Every once in a while Cade looked back at me when we were stuck in traffic. He placed his hand on top of mine, and kissed the back of it before jetting down open streets that turned dry as the black sky faded to denim, bringing the excitement to an end.

"That was fun," Kandi said, rubbing her inner thighs after Mike helped her off of his chopper.

A collective silence shared between us. Cade and his friend glanced at each other, then a curve raised on the side of Mike's mouth. He bounced his bike backwards down the sidewalk near the entrance, while Cade placed his bike in park, and turned around to face me.

We shut the world out around us. His warm hands brushed my legs as they made their way towards my waist. His lecherous eyes hypnotized me.

"You had a good time tonight?" His raspy voice stimulated the raging hormones screaming inside of me.

"I did."

He licked his lips. "I got you back in one piece. Like I said I would."

"You better had, or I would have found the Cosby Kid and asked him to beat you up."

"That was wild, right?" He chuckled.

"It was."

We laughed together.

"That moment will be ours forever." He inched closer to me and gazed into my eyes.

'*Ours? So it's not just me feeling something between us.*'

He leaned forward and placed his silky, full lips on mine. I puckered up and stopped breathing, listening to the soft thump of my heart beating inside of my ears.

My pulse increased with every second our tongues coiled.

Chills covered my entire body, while butterflies swarmed my chest and the pit of my stomach. I hadn't felt that feeling in a long time, but there they were, dancing in the upper part of my chest as I got carried away with lustful emotions in front of an audience.

The moment I had been waiting for all night had finally arrived. It was beautiful. Sweet. Tender. Exhilarating. It felt like my first kiss had been upgraded. How a first kiss should feel. Passionate, paced, perfect, and pure.

A light *smack* resounded between us when our lips parted ways. We stood there staring into each other's eyes, breathing each other in, locking our lips together, and coiling our tongues in each other's mouths in public with zero shame.

His hands clutched onto my waist and I threw my arms around his shoulders. Beneath a fleeting moon and a slim crowd of voyeurs, we tasted each other, fevered in a heat of passion I didn't want to burn out.

Cade pulled back and moaned. "Sweetness."

"Yes."

He turned towards Kandi standing near the dimly lit No Vacancy sign. "I think I brought you to the wrong hotel."

"I know you did."

His face leaned into mine. "You coming with me?"

"You want me to come with you?"

Cade signaled to Mike. "Walk her friend to her room! Make sure she gets in safe!"

Kandi shouted, "Really J.C.!"

Mike parked his bike and walked towards the steps outside of the lobby. Kandi sucked her teeth loud enough for me to hear—

ogling me with either disapproval or jealousy. It was hard to tell from a distance, and I didn't care. I was caught up in Cade's gaze, aroused from the feel of his hands stroking the side of my face.

Shouts from passersby and renters on their balconies screamed at us. "Get a room!" We released the intertwining of our lips and chuckled at the commentary.

Mike returned and led the way back to their hotel. My mind questioned my decision, while my heart fluttered, desperately wanting to partake in the debauchery set in motion.

This behavior was unlike me. I was no saint, but I had never been this bold...This free...This easy. And I had no idea what I was in for.

Chapter 2
The Sweetest Taboo

I wrapped my legs around him as he lifted me from the bike. "I'm watching you. I won't let you get burned." His light, golden brown face grinned resting next to mine. "I've got to hurry up and get you inside."

I squealed as he gently bit my neck.

Mike interrupted us. "Juke, what's your girl's name?"

"Sweetness." Cade laughed, placing me on my feet.

"J.C.," I answered.

"You sure those girls are your friends?" Mike asked, pushing his motorcycle in the back of a trailer connected to a Silverado.

I scowled. "Why would you ask me that?"

Mike raised his brows. "You might want to watch your back is all I'm saying."

"Thanks for the heads up."

My mind wondered what Mike overheard as Cade pushed his bike in the trailer. He tapped my leg and woke me from the trance I was in trying to figure out what I could have done to cause bad blood so early on the trip.

"You ready to go inside." Cade grabbed my hand.

I nodded, and followed him inside a less than stellar homestyle suite. A million questions came to mind regarding his selection of places to lodge, and being a person who wears her emotions on her face, Cade read my mind.

"Not up to your standards?"

"It's okay." I lied.

He snickered. "I didn't book the rooms. Our entire club is staying in this shithole."

"You said it. I didn't."

"Trust me. Your face gave an entire statement."

I set aside my five star taste for a five star night of passion I hoped would come. It was the only thing that could make sleeping in that room worth the trouble. Then I turned around.

"Do y'all hear someone snoring?" I pointed towards the bedroom.

Mike and Cade looked at each other big-eyed.

"Fuck!" Cade whispered below his breath.

"Juke, you know we're not going to be able to wake him," said Mike. "I was gonna crash on the couch, but I'll go next door just in case you get him up." Mike followed Cade into the bedroom, then stormed out with his bag draped over his shoulder. He smirked at me. "Good luck. You might want to lock this door behind me."

I turned the bolt and plopped down on the sofa, pinning my feet at my side. Cade resurfaced minutes later with a look of despair on his face. He stood in the middle of the living room wiping his face with his hands.

"Mike wished me good luck. Do I need it?"

He shook his head. "We both do."

"Well, I don't want to cause any issues. I can take a cab back to my hotel."

"Nah. It's nothing like that. It's just one of my roadies checked in while we were out and already crashed in one of the beds. He gets so drunk, there is no use in trying to wake him. I was in there trying my damnedest, and as you can hear." He pointed to snores coming from the room.

"So are we supposed to sleep on this sofa?"

"It's another bed in the room, but...damn."

"You wanna try this tomorrow? I would offer my room, but it has other women in it whom I don't want to share you with, and according to Mike, I need to feed with a long handle spoon."

Cade smiled at me. "You don't want to share me with your friends?" He sat next to me and laughed. "I'm just fuckin' witchu."

"Of course you are." I looked at him sternly. "But in all seriousness, it seems I'm up here without any friends."

He sat me on his lap and lowered his voice. "I'm your friend."

My head leaned against his. "I hope so."

We reignited the fire from the parking lot of the hotel. I was immersed in passion like a sunburst in the sky, high on curiosity of what this man was about to do to my needy, aching body.

I was lost in him, lost in the moment, and I didn't know why. And as the bulge below my thigh tightened, I felt the seat of my bathing suit grow warm and wet.

I wondered, 'Why am I willing to abandon my self-respect for this man? Why do I trust him? What is going on with me? More importantly, why do I want what is about to happen so badly?'

As his hands rubbed my back with a gentle stroke down the center then molded into a firm press in the dip above my ass, the questions of my desire ran rampant in my head until I caved into the craving. I shuddered from the touch of his fingertips drawing lines up and down my spine, while I rocked my hips to visions of his twitching cock thrusting hard between my thighs.

His hands found their way to my breasts and lifted my bikini top. His trophy colored eyes stared at me, taming me for the moment we both wanted. As they held mine in a trance of desperate debauchery, he stuck out his long tongue, then licked my nipple, reading my response to his seductive gaze. My lips parted, my pussy convulsed, and I creamed myself. And from the smug look on his face, he knew it.

Our moment was underway, my fantasy about to come true. Being forthright about experiencing this new freedom of sexual exploration burning in my veins was a lot to take in, but it was better than living through imprisoned thoughts I'd touch myself to in the heat of the night.

Watching Cade tend to me surpassed any of the impure visions dancing in my head. The careful way he slithered about— gliding from one breast to the other, pinching, nibbling, licking, and teeth grazing my brown nipples.

Near an innocent expression of orgasmic stimulation, I gyrated in his lap, growing impatient to feel him inside my warmth. But he wasn't in a rush.

He took his time exploring the hills on my chest, caressing my neck, and skimming my shoulders. A moan left my mouth as he lowered my face to his, breathing in my gratifying moans, then he kissed me.

"There isn't a hotel on this beach with a vacancy. And we need our own private room." His kisses stole nearly all of the air in my mouth. "What do you want to do?"

I sighed with a breaking voice. "I think you know the answer to that question?"

"I like you, girl. But I don't want to bend you over this couch our first time."

'Please bend me over this couch. I'm begging you.'

I lowered his lips back to my bosom. "So what do you suggest?"

He kissed the path between my bared bosoms, then buried his head into my chest. "Let's go to bed." He heavily sighed. "My cock-blocking ass friend will wake up in a few hours and hit the strip with the rest of the club. Then I'll have you all to myself."

"You sure?"

"I ain't happy, but I'm sure. I can't do you like this."

I was impressed. Also convinced this bloke really did take a liking to me. There I was willing to be plowed on a sofa in a two star hotel, and he thought more of me than I thought of myself. It was sweet, but didn't stop the dirty images in my head of him fucking me on the balcony, or up against the wall, outside on top of his bike in that hot ass trailer, or on the dirty hotel carpet. I wanted to experience him. But it would have to wait.

He took my hand and sat me on the bed. I leaned back and watched him undress, snickering at the snores from his friend.

"Which side do you sleep on?" he asked.

I crawled towards the wall. "This side tonight. Gotta make sure I don't wake up in a sandwich."

"He's harmless." He pointed over his shoulder. "Plus, you said you aren't sharing me, and I for damn sure ain't sharing you."

We nestled under the covers, me still in my bathing suit, and Cade in a wife beater and briefs. When the snores roared loud like a bear, we giggled between light conversation. The sexual tension between us was too high to fall asleep. With every laugh we both made subtle moves, inching closer and closer until the comfort of his dick was pressed between my ass cheeks.

Our bodies rubbed against one another, building enough friction to start a fire. Cade nibbled on the back of my neck, saturating my shoulders with wet laps of his soft, open-mouthed kisses. The strap of my bikini slipped past my biceps and his lips found a new place to graze his teeth. I had never had a man run a combination of light teeth sweeps and smooth kisses to trace my shoulders, or my neck, or the centerline of my back down to the end of my spine.

Beneath the covers he teased me. I turned onto my stomach, and enjoyed the double play of kisses and massages with my eyes focused on the other bed.

The sleeping bear continued to wheeze louder than my moans, and I trusted Cade told me the truth that he would not wake up for a few hours.

Confident my first time with a stranger wouldn't be accompanied by a voyeur witnessing me getting my back blown out, I let go of my inhibitions. I closed my eyes, and accepted that what I craved all evening was going to happen with another body in the room.

I rolled over to my back as he slid the other strap of my top down my arm. Hovering above me and looking into my eyes, he nudged his nose against mine, then kissed me gently. I drew in his tongue, and pulled his chest next to mine to run my hands up and down his contoured back.

'Damn he's a good kisser,' I said to myself, caught up in the rapture of heat and hedonistic dreams.

Cade slivered back to my peaked mounds and toyed with them, rotating between a combination of tongue and finger play. The seat of my bikini became drenched. I wiggled to remove them so he could enter with easy access, but he placed his hand on mine and said, "I want to take them off."

My hands fell to my side as I jerked from a slow tongue stroll tickling my stomach.

"You on the pill?"

"No." I sat up. "I hope you have rubbers."

"I do. But I just marked you with my tongue in case the condom breaks. What I put in that pussy tonight will be mine."

I scoffed. "You seem eager to do me in here, but not in the other room. Why?"

"Who knows how many asses that couch has seen. I know these sheets are clean."

I didn't argue. I was stuck on him like a deer caught in headlights. He leaned over and grabbed a box of condoms from the nightstand.

'So he knew he was getting action on this trip, huh? Of course he was. Look at him. I'll be lucky if I see him after he digs me out.'

His friend's snoring drowned out the sound of the wrapper

being torn open. I watched the silhouette of his brown body roll the latex down his dick, and trembled when it smacked at the base.

"Don't get excited," he whispered, folding my bikini into a roll and sliding it past my feet.

He lifted my ankles and placed them on his shoulders. Side to side he kissed every part of my legs with delicate pecks until he reached my inner thigh. The skillset he displayed when kissing my mouth was now upon my sweet spot. My pussy jittered and spat in his mouth. He moaned and played with it, spreading it around my thighs with his lips and a double thumb roll.

I lost the ability to conceal my moans. I covered my face with a pillow to muffle my shrieks of joie de vivre from my ass being caressed and squeezed and rolled upward off the bed for an open buffet. Cade face fucked my pussy like he was bobbing for apples, or sampling a charcuterie board.

Every part of me was nibbled, licked, savored and sucked. My fingers slipped trying to grasp onto his low-cut, wavy hair as my drip trickled down my ass.

My second coming didn't slow him down. He tapped on my hood then traced my perineum with his tongue. I moaned into the pillow, trembling.

He rose and removed the pillow from my face. "Don't hide that pretty face from me."

Winding my hips forward as his thumbs rubbed the zone on each side of my drenched, pulsing exterior, my eyes met his in the dim light.

"You're spoiling me," I whispered.

"I want to." He smiled. "How old are you, Sweetness?"

Before I answered, he plunged inside my pussy. The gasp of delight that left his mouth satisfied my ego. I inhaled, closed my eyes, and held my breath, counting the seconds before the pain turned to pleasure.

He lowered his torso and his chest to mine. "Open your eyes, Sweetness," he said, pounding me into the cheap sheets.

I obeyed his command, melting at him calling me Sweetness, and the intense look of revelry in his eyes gazing down on me.

"I gave you the right nickname. You are sweet as fuck and your pussy tastes like cotton candy. Here, see for yourself."

Cade was crossing off a lot of firsts for me. I had never gone home with a man I just met, I'd never engaged in coitus with a third party present, and I was clueless to what I tasted like. He changed that, tonguing me down as I gasped in his mouth from the vigorous strokes of his girthy pipe exploring my foundation.

I held on to his shoulders, groaning beneath the boisterous snores of the man a few feet away, hoping he didn't wake up and interrupt the pleasure being gifted to me. Cade and I were so in sync, he read the concerned look on my face.

"He ain't waking up, but if he does I can't stop, Sweetness."

My pussy clenched tighter around his dick, and he groused. I squeezed my walls again and thrust my hips forward.

"Fuck, girl." He exclaimed in a nervous whisper. "You tryin' to see if we can wake him up?"

His compliment boosted my ego. I pushed his head to my breasts, and he adored me with his talented lips, softly pulling on my nipples. His hands rolled around my ass and slid to the back of my knees. He raised them and pressed them next to my head so his dick could dive deeper into my stomach.

Loudly, I squealed and reached for the pillow.

He smacked it away. "Un uh, I want to see your pretty face when you come."

"I might scream."

He kissed me. "So scream." He clasped my bottom lip between his teeth and held his cock on a pressure point. "Let me see you wake him up."

I released a sharp exhale and shook my head no. His slow,

composed strokes transformed into delightful, violent thrusts. I covered my mouth with my hands and wailed in disbelief that I was in bed with a handsome stranger. A thoughtful, attentive, thrill seeker reveling in my warm embrace.

I expected he would treat me like a savage whore once my knickers were off. Deep down, I secretly wanted him to. To pound me into the mattress as if his wood was the stick used to beat my pussy like it was his drum.

It was inexplicable the way I yearned to be manhandled by him. To treat him like a gorgeous field hand at my disposal with orders to plow my garden, and fuck me like the bad girl I was not raised to be.

Cade overpowered me, removing my hands from my mouth with ease. "I told you I want to see your face when you come. Let it out, Sweetness."

I placed my forehead against his shoulder, holding my breath, overcome with pressure and pleasure claiming ownership of my frenzied body.

"Let me hear it," he ordered.

I delivered, exhaling a squeal of joy in between staggered breaths, squeezing his shoulders as he jutted deeper between my watery abyss.

"Oh God." I blasphemed.

"I'm not him." He sucked on my cheek as the tip of his wood spread. His voice turned raspy. "If you're with him right now, tell him I said thank you."

I was too relaxed to pinch him for telling such a bad joke, too weary to laugh at it, and too far gone to care if my outburst woke Teddy Ruxpin on the other side of the room.

Cade grunted when he filled the bag. Our bodies were bound together, his hips to my ass, and my eyes set on his. His mouth popped open as his eyes squinched looking down at me, then his shoulders locked, and his back lengthened strong and tall.

I was his prisoner as he came. His cock bolted us together like a nail screwed into a wall, forcing my walls to shiver from the beautiful painting he hung inside of me.

Cade hovered above me and smiled. "Damn girl, I didn't see you coming this weekend." His tongue licked my lips before he kissed me, then he rolled behind me. "I'm too spent to get you a t-shirt. Sleep in this." He handed me the tank he was wearing.

Padlocked in his arms, I fell asleep holding his hand on soiled sheets with my ass bare and free next to his sticky cock.

Hours later I woke, still wrapped in Cade's arms, tucked beneath the covers. My eyes opened wide when I realized the noise was louder outside than it was in the room.

We were in the quiet. Bike engines and balding tires faintly screeched from the street, neighbors laughed obnoxiously from their balconies, and deep male voices conversed from the living room. But what concerned me more was the stifling sound of silence on the other side of the room.

'What happened to the poor bastard snoring?'

I wondered if I had been exposed, or worse— photographed while I was asleep. Had the male voices in the living room taken a sneak peak of my naked body on display, and Cade covered me sometime in the night? I freaked out and tapped his hand to wake him.

He groaned and squirmed. "Sweetness. I'm so glad you didn't skip out on me. I would have thought last night was a dream if you weren't in my arms right now." He pressed his morning wood between my bum.

"You still got me?"

He sat up and lifted the back of my hand to his mouth. "Want me to show you?" His dick trembled on my ass and his hand slipped between my slit.

The door opened.

"Damn. My bad. I was hoping you were still asleep. I need to grab something out of my bag." His friend giggled. "I fixed breakfast. Left some for you and your friend."

"We're fine."

His friend whispered. "Who is she?"

"Man get your shit and go!" Cade fussed.

"I'm going. She got any friends?"

Cade sighed. "And sleep on the couch tonight!"

"The couch?"

Cade threw a pillow at his friend. "Just go!"

"Nice meeting you. Juke, we're waiting on you to ride out." He slammed the door.

I burst into laughter.

Cade tickled the back of my shoulder with his lips and palmed my shaven patch. "What's so funny?"

"Nothing," I said. "Sometimes I laugh when I'm nervous."

He flipped me over to my back and pinned me down to the bed. "I want you again."

I moaned. "I want you, too, but can I shower and get the muck from last night's air, and our residue off of me first?"

"Sounds good, but how 'bout we pick up where we left off tonight. You gonna hang out with me again?"

"That would be nice."

I showered and finger brushed my teeth while his friends crowned him for topping me last night. The cheers and jaunts from the other room embarrassed me before I took my walk of shame, but I smiled through it and covered myself in one of Cade's oversized t-shirts and boxer shorts, tied at the side of my waist.

As I waited for him to finish grooming, I told myself I would never see him again.

'He is not going to pick you up later today. He will move on to the next easy lay, so accept this for what it was, be cool, and don't be this fucking stupid ever again.'

Cade rejoined me in the bedroom, emerging through the doors

with steam surrounding him like a smoke machine at a concert. "Don't go out there without me." He pointed to the living room area.

"I wouldn't dare," I said, searching between the sheets for my bathing suit.

The smell of mountains, cool water, and mint trailed behind him as he walked around the room. The aroma led me to regret my earlier decision to postpone a second round to shake the sheets.

I sat on the bed ready to view the image of him dripping wet without a towel, thinking we could sneak in one quiet round before we parted ways.

"Did I take too long in there?"

I smiled. "Who am I to complain? You're my ride."

"What are you and your friends getting into today?"

"I have no idea," I said, studying his muscular physique, shining from freshly applied aftershave and lotion. "Just call me when you wanna hook up tonight."

He pulled me up and kissed me, then threw on some clothes and grabbed his keys. "Let's ride."

He held my hand and escorted me through the living room where some of his crew was waiting. They introduced themselves, some with nods and some with smiles, giving Cade thumbs up of approval when they assumed I wasn't paying attention.

As a group, we joined the rowdy members of the club gathered outside. They catcalled, whistled, and shamed the fuck out of me by praising Cade for his score. It was the ugliest moment of the past 24 hours until he silenced them.

One of them yelled, "Juke, those your shorts? They look better on her!"

Cade stopped short on the steps. "Watch your fucking mouth, man."

"I know you ain't came to the beach and fell in love!"

The club members snickered and I lowered my head.

"Ignore him, Juke. He just mad he ain't pull her." A male voice said over the rumble.

"And he couldn't." I added.

Taunts and jokes flew at us like center targets on a dart board.

Cade pulled me in close and kissed me in front of his crew. "I like your little sexy, feisty ass."

"I like you, too. Why do they call you Juke?"

"I'll tell you tonight."

I straddled behind my *one knight stand* in shining armor, hugging him tight for the short drive, not wanting to let him go. The pile of bikes turned in the lot of my hotel behind us. They honked their horns, spun their tires, and flamed their exhausts, stirring commotion as we said our goodbyes.

I bounced off Cade's bike, sure it was the last time I would see him.

"Come here, Sweetness." His eyes glistened in the sun. "You can't leave me like that."

"Like what?"

"Without giving me your number."

"I slipped my number in your back pocket. And when you dial that number, make sure you call me by my name."

"I thought you were feeling me up." He chuckled. "And I know your name."

"Do not say Sweetness."

He scoffed, rolled his eyes, then pulled out his phone and showed me an incomplete entry in his contacts.

"What does that say?" He grilled me.

My heart wavered and my body tingled. "It says J.C."

"Now put your number in there so I can give you a spanking later for talking shit."

He gently patted my ass and grinned. *'Damn,'* I thought. He had made it hard for me to walk away from him with expectations. I belonged to him at that moment.

The biggest smile grew on my face. "Yes, sir," I said, laughing as I typed in my information.

"I'll be by later to pick you up."

One final kiss to end our night and begin our day left me hopeful, but when he drove away, tension formed in my neck as I entered the lobby of the hotel. I exhaled, bracing myself for the load of drama Mike warned was brewing. And though I was dressed in last night's sin, I still asked God to cover me. Because only he knew what was said about me, and what waited for me in a room full of wolves pretending to be my friends.

Chapter 3
Fear

I had broken rule number one— Never take a man home from the club and expect him to be lying next to you in the morning. In my case I went home with a man during whore's weekend at the beach, but luck was on my side as Cade served as a one-time exception to this rule. As for lessons in friendship, I learned birds of a feather truly do flock together, and the words I spoke to Cade before he dropped me off were in fact true. I was not amongst friends.

The room was colder than ice when I walked inside. Odd stares and smirks greeted me when Kandi let me in. The chatter went from loud enough to hearing them laugh in the hall, to a dead silence where you could clearly hear the waves sweep in from the ocean, and the chirping of seagulls flying near the opened balcony door.

Mike's warning that I should watch my back prepared me for the awkward return, and unfortunately he was right in his assumption. The joy of my spirit was not welcome there, and the amazing night I'd spent with Cade carried in my voice when I attempted to liven up the room.

"Good morning." I smiled.

Kandi's cousin, Katrina, whom I knew was staying with us was the only person to respond.

"Hey, J.C."

"Oh good, you made it. What time did you get in?"

"Around four o'clock, I think. It's a good thing you weren't here though. We were crowded like hell in these small ass beds last night. Well, we were." She pointed to Kandi and a girl I didn't know. "Devaughn and Foxx had it better than us with only two in their bed."

"Sure did." Devaughn cosigned and scowled at me as she stepped out of the bathroom.

I thought to myself. '*She wasted no time to make it clear she has an issue with me. I guess she and Kandi both said nasty things about me in front of Mike last night. And what was Katrina really trying to say to me about the sleeping arrangements?*'

"We're getting ready to head out. You are coming with us, right?" Katrina asked.

"Yeah. I've already showered. I can get changed real quick."

Devaughn butted in. "We ain't heard shit from you all night, now we're supposed to wait for you to get ready?"

"Kandi knew what was up. Her driver walked her up to the room to make sure she got in safe last night. Didn't she tell you?"

My response was overlooked.

"How long is it gonna take for you to get ready?"

"Like five minutes."

Devaughn sighed. "Y'all, let's head out."

The energy was negative, the vibe was toxic, and the day was off to a bad start. As I rummaged through my duffel, Devaughn grumbled below her breath. I pretended not to hear the giggles and whispers travel around the room, refusing to be baited into an argument about nothing.

I'd gone from the happiest I had been in months, to embarrassed, shamed, and outcasted. I would have never thought sleeping in a room feet away from a snoring drunk was ideal, but after the icy return to my frenemies, I was grateful for the turn my wild night took.

I held back tears as my chest heaved of hurt. I had nowhere to go except with them, no one to call to rescue me, and pennies in my purse that wouldn't buy a bus ticket home after giving the girls my part for the hotel room.

After a few deep breaths, I pinned my bob behind my ears, faked a smile, and hit the streets with my foes and woes.

The routine was almost the same as last night— Pose next to cute guys on bikes, flirt, and crash cookouts. The difference was Devaughn led our whereabouts, selected which bike clubs drove us around, and picked the parties we swung by. And to keep the peace, I kept quiet.

I couldn't enjoy the day as I had the night before. The planned weekend of fun took a turn for the worse, and I was clueless as to why. With Devaughn being my transportation home, I was forced to grin and bear the eye rolls, cheap shots, and disrespect of being left out of conversations amongst the group.

My mind was frazzled as I swallowed my suppressed, growing rage. The pent up hostility lured me outside the beachside tent party we crashed, where out of desperation, I called cousins, friends I hadn't spoken to in a while, and ex-boyfriends known never to miss Bike Week, in search of an alternate way home, and a place to sleep— Unlucky in my pursuits.

When I returned to the party, I sat near the sand bar. A man raised his hand to get the bartender's attention.

"Can I buy you a drink to get that mean look off yo' face?"

"No, thank you." I cracked a minimal smile.

Devaughn walked up and slapped my hand. "The fuck is you

doing? You don't turn down free drinks. Bitch, next time somebody asks you, you better tell them you want a Henny and Coke." She sucked her teeth and walked away.

"If you're here with her, I see why your face looks like that." The man added.

I raised my brows.

"You sure you don't want anything?" he asked.

"A way home would be nice."

"I can't help you there." He handed the bartender twenty dollars and ordered a beer. "Keep the change and give her whatever she wants." He looked at me. "You be easy, Slim."

The man grabbed his beer and walked away. The bartender looked at me flat-eyed. I pressed my lips together.

"What can I get you?"

"A water, please."

"Your credit can get you something stronger than that."

"I don't drink alcohol."

"Then what are you doing out here?"

"Making a lot of damn mistakes it seems."

"Been there. I'll get you that water."

Holding a bottle of water around a crowd of heavy drinkers is a sure way to attract attention. Men approached me at the bar with offers to put a real drink in my hand to the point it became worrisome and exhausting, but not as exhausting as Devaughn.

She circled back with Kandi. "This bitch gotta water in her hands. Why are you so fuckin' lame?"

I shook my head and exhaled sharply.

"I'm a ask this bartender if you turned down any drinks. If he says yes, I'm a beat your ass." She squeezed between two patrons waiting for their order. "You!" She pointed to the bartender. "Did anybody ask her if she wanted a drink?"

He peered at DeVaughn then over to me. "Is there something you want?"

"A Henny and Coke. One of these moneybags rightchea is buying."

"Bitch, I ain't buying your drunk ass shit," said one of the men she squeezed between.

"This party is full of lames. Let's bounce."

I knew Kandi longer than I had known Devaughn, so when she laughed at her bullying me, Mike's warning came to fruition. She knew I had to be pushed into violence, and had been around me long enough to know how uncouth I could be after letting my anger build. It bothered me that she thought whatever was happening was funny, but to prevent myself from being stranded, I continued to hold my tongue.

My chest burned from the cry I swallowed, having to be a weak link for the sake of a ride home, and despite my wonderful night, I regretted going on the trip.

When we left the party I walked behind the girls with my eyes planted on my phone, missing the action and attractions on the strip. The phone tower signals were hit and miss, so when I saw I had one missed call on the screen, my heart skipped hoping it was Cade calling to rescue me from the drama.

The call was from Kool, my male best friend. The one person I could always count on when I found myself in a sticky situation. His message stated, *'I have a few reservations on North and South Myrtle. Hit me up if you still need one. Just hit me up anyway. I don't like the way you sound.'*

My face lit up brighter than the hot sun beaming down on us. DeVaughn didn't like that.

"The fuck you so happy for?" She frowned.

"No reason."

"Stop frontin' like that man from last night called you. You ain't never gonna see him again." DeVaughn and Kandi slapped hands, cackling at my expense.

"Who says it was him?" I sipped my water.

They looked at each other and scowled their faces.

"By the way, I need a key to the room," I said to them.

"What for?"

My patience began to wear thin. "Why do I have to say? I paid my money."

"Nah, bitch. We might not see your ass again, and I'm not losing deposit money on a key."

"Why are y'all giving me shit?"

The two of them stared at each other while the other girls swayed off to the side.

I looked Devaughn in the eyes. "And why do you care so much about my hookup from last night?"

Devaughn's voice grew loud. "You just hopped on that dude's bike like it wasn't shit! With no regard to us! We had to follow yo' ass and put up with some lame, broke motherfuckers! We should have all decided if we wanted to go with them."

"Like we did today? I don't recall having a say in whose bikes we rode on to get to this party. I haven't complained once." I pointed out.

"And we were all looking at that dude," Kandi added.

I couldn't hide my smirk. Kandi had revealed the truth behind the animosity. This wasn't the first time she and I were interested in the same guy, but it was the first time her prancing back and forth in front of one so she could be chosen didn't work. And the first time she said it out loud.

In the past it was always the elephant in the room that we never spoke on. If a guy liked me, she flirted with him. She would go out of her way to be seen, keel over at stale comedy, and casually slip in a negative about me, then pretend she was just kidding around.

What Kandi didn't know was that one of her previous boy toys spent a lot of time standing on my porch telling me about all of the dirty things she would say about me, then beg me to give him a chance. But I never wanted her sloppy seconds, though she was content with mine, getting off from the feeling of slighting me somehow.

Whereas I chose not to believe what her boyfriend said about her was true, assuming he was just an asshole feeding me lies so we would fuck, she indeed was a backstabbing bitch.

I huffed. "I didn't know we were all looking at my guy. I thought we were looking at all of them."

DeVaughn rolled her eyes. "You know what you did was fucked up."

"Actually, I don't. Y'all hook up with dudes all the time. The both of you have left me in clubs straggling a ride home to go lay up. So is the problem I got lucky, or the fact I was chosen by the best looking one?"

DeVaughn's wood smoking voice overshadowed mine. "See that's that smart-mouthed shit I don't like right there."

I reveled inside that I hit a nerve, and was tickled that the both of them were mad Cade's friends didn't want to continue the night with them, so they projected their rejection onto me.

My screen lit up and I held up my hands. "I'll catch up with y'all later."

Devaughn sucked her teeth. "Run away. Scared ass."

Chapter 1
Paradise

It didn't take a genius to see where that conversation was headed. And Devaughn was right, I was scared. And you know what they say, scared people kill people. I'll leave it at that.

Biting my tongue was the first level of my restraint to not explode and expose their secrets to the public. If I had announced in front of everyone that Kandi goes around fucking all of her friend's and cousin's boyfriends to hold it over their head, and how Devaughn has been scheming to screw her landlord when she can't make rent every other month, we would have been brawling like cats and in jail.

Luckily for all of us, I re-centered and removed myself before the nothing burger of an argument escalated to a point of no return.

I stepped away from the ridiculousness those two idiots cooked up, and answered my incoming call. "Hey. Where are you?"

"Coming up on your hotel. You there?"

"I wish. I'm stranded somewhere on the north side."

"Stranded?" Cade's voice cracked with concern. "You want me to come rescue you?"

"Like yesterday."

"Give me a landmark."

"I'm sitting in front of Surfside Pointe Resort."

"Be there in about twenty minutes."

I sat on the stone wall of the resort's walkway during my wait. A strong grain of marijuana polluted the air as stoners took turns passing a joint around on the other side of the wall. The girls hung by close so I could see them, and took turns looking in my direction. Then Kool called and ripped into me.

"What the fuck, J.C. I told you to hit me back." His voice hits below soprano as he chastises me.

"I was going to." I explained. "Kool, I should have listened to you and stayed home."

He kissed his teeth. "I tried to tell you. This is not your scene."

"*Welllll*— actually, I met someone. He seems nice."

"No, you haven't met anyone worthwhile up here. It's all a game. Every man up here is pretending to be something they are not. And nice ain't it. Watch yourself."

"He says he's a ball player. His friends call him Juke. Ever heard of him?"

"Nah. He's probably lying. Sounds like you met a douche. Some wannabe with failed NFL dreams. Fuck him."

I laughed. "I'll look him up when I get home."

Distracted with my phone call, I failed to notice the girls walking towards me. I paused my conversation as they walked by. The loud music playing from the cars parading in the street, and a portable CD player from one of the renters muted what they were saying to each other. But I read Devaughn's lips as she stared at me while whispering to Kandi. "Stupid bitch gon' be waiting out here all night."

I sighed. "Speaking of home. I think I may need a lift, so don't leave from up here without talking to me first, please?"

"What's going on, Babes? Who did you come up here with?"

"Kandi and DeVaughn." I mumbled.

"After I told you not to? Are you glutton for punishment? We gotta have a long talk when we get back."

"No we don't. I have learned my lesson. Several of them."

"That explains why you sound like you wanna cry."

"I deserve all the smoke. I know. I'll fill you in when I figure out a way to get my stuff out of the room. The front desk won't give me a key since my name isn't on the reservation, and those bitches won't give me one."

"Swing by my hotel on the south side. I'll leave a key at the desk. But J.C. This is for you only. I didn't book extra rooms for another motherfucker to get laid on my dime."

I burst into laughter. "I wouldn't do you like that. Always my lifesaver, Kool."

"Be careful. And watch your back."

Sifting through the crowds on and off the street, I exhaled relief. All I needed to do was make it through the night, and get home tomorrow.

Cade revved the engine of his bike when he pulled up in front of the hotel.

I hopped off the wall and hurdled my legs around him. "Thanks for saving me."

"You know I can't drive with you on me like this." He laughed then gave me a kiss. "What's wrong?"

"I'll tell you later." I shrugged off my hurt feelings and put a smile on my face. "I didn't think I'd see you this early."

"Believe it or not, all I did today was think about you. What you wanna do?"

"Just hang out with you."

"You hungry?"

"I could go for a pizza."

"She wants pizza in Calabash City." He shook his head with a curve on his lips. "Whatever you want. Let's go, Sweetness."

Cade gripped my ass as I spun around him. A tingly sensation covered my body whole once I smelled the cool, watery musk fading on his neck. I squeezed his chest as he cracked the muffler to work our way into the stalled traffic.

"What happened to your friends?" I asked.

"They cut out early. Said this shit was wack."

"What's your take?"

"If I hadn't met you, I would have cut out with them."

I squeezed him tighter. "I'm suddenly glad I failed to find a ride home a few hours ago."

He eased his bike further towards the light. "So you were gonna leave without seeing me?"

"I wasn't sure you were gonna call me. And I'm in a bit of a bind with the girls I'm staying with. They've been dogging me all day, and saying shit out of pocket because I stayed with you last night."

"The chicks from last night?"

"Yup. Your friend Mike didn't lie about them."

"I was wondering why you were by yourself when I pulled up. They don't know shit about me. Did they leave you up here on this side?"

"Look to your right. It's more heat coming my way from the sidewalk than this street."

Cade glanced into the walking crowd and chuckled. He looked at me over his shoulder and said, "Give me a kiss before the light changes."

I stood on the pegs as he leaned his head back. We shared a quick, soft, intimate kiss then took off on the cleared path in front of us.

In the center of town we found a local pizzeria.

"Unpopular opinion. I think mom and pop pizza spots are better than chains," I said.

"I can do you one better. Unpopular opinion. Digiorno can give chain pizzas a good run."

"One night we'll have to do a taste test and get fat together. If you promise not to judge me after."

"I won't. And I'll put a wager on it."

"Bet."

Nothing about that weekend should have been romantic, but it was. He was. Feeding me slices of cheesy pie at an outside table under a whirring air conditioned vent, wiping grease from the side of my mouth with a napkin while seducing me with his cat eyes, and holding me close to him to steal kisses during one of my long rants. He said he didn't see me coming the night before. I felt the same spending time with him alone and away from the chaos, the excitement, and the crowds. He was the excitement for me, and I fell in love.

At twenty-one, I didn't know what those four letters meant. I thought it was just a word to throw around when you felt confused by lust in heated moments. But this felt like something more. Something I couldn't turn off. Someone I couldn't get enough of.

"If I looked up Jaya Marcel, would I find you?" He bit the last slice of pizza.

"Why do I feel like you already have?"

He pouted his lips like Bobby Dinero and shrugged his shoulders. I avoided his eyes and played with the crust of my last slice.

"I'm not listed if that's what you mean. But if I sent some of my music to you via mail, you'd have my address. Unfortunately, it wouldn't reach you with just the name Cade on the envelope."

"My last name is Williamson."

"Cade Williamson." I turned towards him. "That sounds made up."

He pulled out his license and flicked it. "Mail it to this address, Chanelle Marcel."

I gave him a once over. "That's why I go by J.C."

He handed me the pen from the check folder and the duplicate receipt. I wrote down his information and tucked the folded slip in the side pocket of my bag.

"Why do they call you Juke? I mean I have an idea, but I hope I'm wrong."

He faked a cough. "You make me laugh with that slick mouth."

"So, I'm right?"

'Please say it ain't so.'

He cleared his throat. "It's a nickname from high school. I was known to fake out the defense. They would think I was going one way, then I'd switch it up and sidestep in another direction." He mimicked the mannerism in which he would move on the field.

"So you're a decepticon?"

He cackled at my joke. "I like that. Too late for it to stick, but that's a good one."

"Well if I ever call you Juke, it won't be for your footwork."

He stopped chewing. "My dick just got hard." His eyes twinkled in the center.

The ride back to his place was peaceful. I rested my head against the contour of his toned shoulder and allowed myself to be swept away in the moment holding him in my arms. I couldn't deny our chemistry. Whether fake or real, a bond was forming between us. My wild heart was mending with his on our ride, and I felt beautiful. Wanted and desired. And I was no warrior against the fate of love. So I didn't fight it.

We were finally alone and overdue for a sheet shag. Cade carried me into the bedroom and threw me on the mangled bed.

"No turndown service this weekend?" I joked.

Our lips *smacked*, and *smacked*, and *smacked* as the passion inside of me burst at my core. The black strings on my hips became untied with a delicate, slow brush of his fingers. He gazed at me with illicit pleasure blazing in his eyes with full, puckered lips pecking on mine as he pleased.

"What kind of voodoo you put on me, Sweetness? I heard what they do from 'round your way."

"Well they must do it where you're from, too, because I find myself feeling something strong when I'm with you." I bit his lip. "You've been the highlight of this messed up weekend for me."

"This is crazy, right?" He kissed me and pulled back, glossing me over with an intense look in his eye. "I'm gonna shut up and make love to you now. We can finish this conversation later."

"I'd like that very much."

My bikini top flew onto the other bed. My pussy thrusted upwards against Cade's shorts.

"Hold on, baby, I gotta get them off first." He snickered.

"Hurry up," I ordered, pulling his shirt above his head.

The pounding of his heart beat against my palms, and the chaos exploding inside of me was briefly tamed as a mixture of flutters crowded my chest. The feeling was more than carnal lust.

He looked down at me with a tenderness in his eyes. "Do I need to go in the drawer?"

I shook my head. "No." Eager to have his twitching dick between my legs and hear his raspy voice celebrate conquering me.

His golden eyes turned brighter at my permission to proceed without caution. The flutters raced from my chest and to my head, urging me to withdraw my consent, but I didn't listen. I knew I was being stupid and making the biggest mistake of my life, but I could not control my desire to feel him without the friction. I wanted to give myself to him. Completely.

I was frightened and behaving irresponsibly. But I was also taken by his masculinity, his interest in me, and found myself undeniably swept. As my mind screamed at me from the depths of my soul to backtrack my last statement, I shut out that inner voice and lost myself in the moment.

My lover stood at the edge of the bed stripped to full glory. I breathed out of anticipation, biting my nails, and squirming out of my bikini bottoms as he palmed his penis and stroked it with one hand.

He smiled at me. "You are sexy. You know that?"

"Maybe." I leaned back, getting turned on further at the sight of his fingers rubbing below the hood of his cock.

"Quit fucking around. You know it."

I shrugged. "That's not what you really want to say right now, is it?"

"I'm thinking."

I perked up. "About what?"

"If *Imma* be able to pull out. Just looking at you I know I'm not."

I knew I had fallen hard when the following words flew out of my mouth.

"If you don't, you don't. We can figure that out later."

Cade stepped forward and dropped to his knees. The conversation ended with my legs being pulled forward and placed on his shoulders. He slurped and trilled on my pussy like it was foam on a latte. The thirsty suction of his mouth drinking from my fountain with twisting tongue play stimulated my quaking center. The raspy whispers of his voice preaching how good I tasted in between spurts for air, fucked up my psyche to think of nothing or no one else but him.

My needs and wants became the same while in his care. I wanted to be fucked. Plucked, pulled apart, and put back together how a surgeon cuts and seals. But Cade felt otherwise. He worshiped my pussy until I pulled the soiled sheets from the corners of the mattress— Giving me a reason to never forget that weekend or him...A reason to dread our fling coming to its end.

My waters dripped down the sides of his mouth onto the carpet. I lifted my head, tickled by his greasy mouth catching shine by the outside light, then I locked my eyes with his. He wiped the shine from his face on my calf, then stood tall above me, lifting my feet to his shoulders. Together, a sharp exhale exchanged between us from the barrier free touch of flesh connecting us at my border.

Towering me from that angle, the light from the street posts rewarded me with glimpses of gold specks around his iris. I stared into them, moaning and wailing from the deep, swirling, slow pounding motion of his ass thrusting his dick between my walls. I rained on him. Came for him. Yearned for him. Burned for him.

His strokes were intricate, and deliberate with a meticulous execution of blended jabs in a sturdy drill pattern. The steadiness of his hips caroused my body to a level of pleasure that not only fucked my pussy, but also fucked my mind. Around the top of my canal he rowed, separating the waves of my waters trickling down on his oar.

"Aggh." A high pitched grunt just below the tone of a soprano expelled from his lips. With ease he spun me over to my stomach. "Get that pretty ass up for me, baby."

I crawled to my knees as warm hands gripped my waist, dragging me back towards the edge. Faced down with my ass up, my pussy throbbed open, clasping when the tip of Cade's dick rolled around my slit. The clay texture of his head rubbing up and down the path to my asshole forced my cheeks to twitch. I inched closer to him every time the tip touched my lips and slipped off.

A villainous growl escaped his throat. "You want this dick, don't you, Sweetness?"

My ass cheeks jiggled and both my holes blossomed and pulsed wide open.

His wet fingers massaged my exit. "Mmm, do that again, babes."

In full control of my organs, my pussy and asshole clapped for him. Cade's lips kissed my cheeks, then trailed over to the center of my bum. He licked my entrance soft and sweet while his fingers circled the crème hanging on the outer layer of my folds. My shoulders tightened as a flush feeling traveled down the line of my back.

His dick slid in. "Umph."

He pulled it out. He slid it back in halfway, holding his shaft with his palm. Then, pulled it back out. My hand balled into a fist and pounded the bed.

"Stay deep," I begged.

Cade's hands cuffed my breasts while he rode me stiff, hard, and slow like before, applying pressure to untouched corners. I squealed into the filthy sheets.

"J.C." He called me. Not Baby, not Sweetness. "I'm coming to see you."

"You better." I sighed between panted breaths.

"But now I'm coming in you." He gurgled. "Ohhh Sweetness! I know that's a boy." His legs shook like he was trying to break the record on the Richter scale. "Ah, ah." He exhaled with his head tilted back. "Fuck yeah, I'm coming to see you, baby."

I should have regretted my decision, should have been ashamed I let him nut in me, and upset I sacrificed my future, and my health for a few minutes of mind blowing, euphoric joy. But I felt none of that.

Looking at him over my shoulder holding his balance with my ass as a handle, I accepted what I had done. I'd fallen into sin and had no qualms about it.

"Either my dick doesn't want to leave your pussy, or she's got one hell of a grip I can get used to."

I loosened my hold of him and giggled. "You are no longer held captive."

"I wasn't complaining. She's acting like she's mine. Is she?"

"That's up to you."

He massaged my legs. "You're mine."

I was tickled pink by his assertiveness and didn't object. He slid between my legs and rested his head on my chest, nibbling on my nipples and rubbing my body from my waist to my neck.

"I don't want to wait for a package in the mail to be able to find you. Make sure you put all of your information in my phone before you say good-bye," he said, in between kisses, then placed our bodies in the center of the bed.

"Is that an order?"

He grinned. "Baby, I'm already thinking about my schedule so I can come see you."

He fell asleep with me entrapped in his embrace, moaning and humming, and twitching his eyes whenever I wiggled to get away. I stared at the clock while I listened to him sleep, afraid the loveliness of the moment could turn sour if I found myself stuck without a way home.

Anxiety took me out of the beauty being tucked away in Cade's arms. My mind raced, wondering how I could manage a short reconciliation with my frenemies to make it home, if they've already left me and my belongings behind, if what I had just done put me in the family way, and if so, how bad would it be.

Then, my mind shifted to the horrors of my body going through changes, screams of labor pains, and fucking up the years of my youth because I couldn't find, or afford a babysitter. I surprised myself and smiled, thinking if I did conceive a child with this man, how beautiful the moment of conception had been. I wasn't abused, berated, or disrespected for one moment, and thought if a child came to be from a beautiful mistake I would love it.

At 5 a.m. I woke him. He grunted and held me tighter in his arms, pretending to sleep through the taps of my fingers to his chest. With all my might, I lifted his muscular arm from around me and hopped out of bed to search the room for my swimsuit.

He yawned. "You leaving me already?"

"It's time."

"One more hour, baby."

"I don't have that. Those heffas would love to leave me stranded up here."

Cade mulled about and covered me with another one of his

shirts. "You're sending me home with lighter luggage." He smiled as he buttoned me up.

"I'll mail your shirts back, or you can have them back when you come see me."

"I went to sleep thinking of when I'm gonna make that trip."

"Hopefully soon." I grabbed a pen and mini notepad from the nightstand.

He watched me pensively as I wrote my information on the pad.

"Next move is on you." I folded the piece of paper and stuck it in his suitcase.

The cold, brisk early morning air slapped my bare legs as I held onto him, burying my face deep in his back, imprinting the smell of his skin to remember him always.

The girls were indeed leaving on time, loading the car in the parking lot. Cade parked a few feet away from them, cursing below his breath.

"You sure you're gonna be alright to ride back with them?"

"I honestly don't know. Can I trust you'll answer your phone if something happens on my way home?"

"I'll answer, but the way those girls are looking at you, I might need to take you to the bus station."

"Cade, one thing I don't do is buses."

"I hear you, but it might be your safest bet."

Kandi shouted across the lot. "Your bags are in the back!"

"I guess that's my cue. Be safe," I said, clinging to his shoulder.

"Shit— baby, you be safe."

We laughed.

He reeled me in close, planting a tender kiss to my lips. "I'll be seeing you."

And I walked away from the sweetest of goodbyes.

Chapter 5
Bring Me Home

My sweet goodbye lasted but a few seconds. A mixture of emotions formed a commotion in my chest as I opened the door of Satan's spawn shuttle. I was happy to have met Cade, sad I was leaving him, and fearful that a fight would leave me stranded on the side of the road.

Cade hadn't cranked his bike before Devaughn showed her ass.

"Get in!" she yelled.

I sighed looking back at him. With raised brows, he sat there, listening to her lash out at me before I could close the back door of her car. I was embarrassed. Ashamed. And fed up.

I lost track of the amount of shits, damns, and fucks she spewed, berating me like a child for the first twenty minutes of the ride home. The holding back of my rage formed tears in my eyes. I huffed to ease the pain of suppressed anger in my chest.

Silence was my golden ticket home at the hand of two she-devils, and by his grace and mercy, I survived the verbal abuse, and toxic lift home with my dignity left somewhere on the side of the Hell's Highway.

By the time we arrived in front of my apartment., the car was quiet. DeVaughn popped the trunk, I grabbed my bags from the back seat, and slammed her trunk shut after grabbing my suitcase. She looked at me with pure evil eyes in the rearview. I returned the same look back at her. I had had enough and made it home which was my goal. And though I was beyond tired and humiliated, I had enough energy left in me to go a round or two if need be.

She stuck her middle finger out of the window and sped off. I returned the gesture and took my first real breath after hours of biting my tongue, went inside my apartment, and leaned against the door.

'Thank you Lord that's over.'

———

He didn't call. I had unpacked, bathed, and wrote about the weekend's highlights with my cell phone in an arm's reach ready to hear his voice. Instead, I found myself tortured from the stillness in my house, and the echoes of Devaughn cackling, "You ain't never gonna see him again," had a field day in my head.

As I sat in the dark of my room processing the previous days of torment and temptation with my hands tucked between my thighs, I pictured Cade's light eyes staring at me. Flashes of the city moving fast while I nestled behind him on his bike, and the lights from the sky wheel brought a smile to my face as the natural scent of his brown skin somehow lit below my nose. I could smell him even though he wasn't there.

The phone rang, and I stopped smiling as if the person on the other line could see me.

"Good, you're back," Thedé said when the line stopped ringing.

"Oh, it's you."

"Well damn, hello to you, too. I guess I was right. You shouldn't have gone with them, innit?"

"Yeah, you were right. I should have stayed my ass home like you did."

"I know you only went 'cause you still hung up on that jackass." She scoffed. "I get it."

"After the weekend I had, I believe I'm over him."

"Uh oh. What did you do?"

A huge smile brightened my face. "Fucked some man who put that juju on me, and now I'm sitting in here with all the lights turned off waiting for him to call."

"Noooooo. You didn't."

"I did."

"You use a condom?"

"The first time."

"Girl! I ought to box yo ass off!" Her voice shifted to a whisper. "You know better than that. You don't even move like that."

"I know."

"Get dressed. We're going out. I remember the last time you stayed up in the house looking at the walls and drove yourself crazy."

"But what if he calls?"

"J.C., really? That motherfucker is not gonna call." She laughed. "I'm sorry, but this is why you can't move like them gal you gone up there with. You get too attached to these assholes, and unfortunately, assholes is all we got left out here to choose from."

I sighed. "I'm tired."

"You'n tired. You want to sit by that phone and hope it rings. Be ready in thirty minutes."

Thedé blew the horn loud enough to wake the neighborhood. The door hadn't fully closed before she commanded me to tell her about my dalliance with danger.

"Promise not to laugh." I shoved her arm.

The car jolted in the middle of the road.

"Girl! Stop playing. And I'm laughing already 'cause you a love struck motherfucker." Thedé guffawed. "Look atcha."

"I have never been tended to as delicate and gentle as a rose petal being plucked, so slow and intense. I can still feel his mild kisses sucking the largest organ of my body in its entirety, snatching my soul and tying it with his."

"Are you writing one of your love songs right now, or are we talking about knocking the boots here?"

I sucked my teeth. "I keep forgetting you're stone cold, so in words you'll appreciate, I let him tap it, he put it on me, and I'm feenin' for more."

"That's all you had to say."

We joined the rest of the locals that either didn't go to the beach, or had returned early at a bar downtown.

"Your girl Kandi is over there eyeing you," Thedé warned.

"I saw her when we came in. Bitch."

"Tell me what happened?"

Unloading the highs and lows over apps and spirits softened my delivery of the theatrics I endured on the trip.

Thedé seethed from her teeth and shook her head. "Fuck both of them. I mean, I'ne got no beef with them, but they did you wrong as hell, and for what? You don't wanna hear it, but Imma say it. I told you not to go with them."

"You're right. I don't want to hear that for the millionth time. And I'm done with them for good. You ain't gotta worry 'bout me."

"Tell me this– How did they act on the way up there?"

"Fine. I guess. We mostly listened to music."

Thedé scoffed. "Please tell me you've figured out that part."

"Because they still needed my money for the room."

"Exactly. Ole using ass dirty bitches." Thedé mean-mugged me. "Enough about them. Fill me in on this man you let raw dog you. Must have been something 'cause you keep looking at your phone."

My head gestured towards the other table. "Those two heffas made me feel lower than low saying he wasn't gonna call me. But he did more than that. He showed up for me. Picked me up right in front of them and showed me a good time."

"He gets one point for that."

"Now, I'm a sitting duck hoping he keeps his word."

"Which is?"

"That we'll see each other again."

Thedé sipped from her straw. "You my girl and I love ya, but highly unlikely. You should have gotten his number, but still, I wouldn't chase behind some random peen I screwed at the beach."

"I do have his number. His address, too. But I'm not calling him first. It's his move."

"Thank God you ain't completely whipped. But what possessed you to trust him to slide in unstrapped?"

I sighed. "I don't know. I can't explain the way I felt around him. Carefree comes to mind."

"And easy," Thedé mumbled below her breath.

I rolled my eyes at her. "As if you haven't given it up on the first night before."

She cleared her throat. "You were saying?"

I paused. "Before someone threw stones from their glass house, I was gonna say I've never felt comfortable with anyone as much as I did with him. It felt like we were kindred spirits or something."

"At bike week? Really, J.C.?"

"Don't make me feel dumber than I already do. I got swept up in the moment, I guess."

"My bad. I'm just in awe how this mofo charmed free panties off of you and has you out here blushing and shit. But then again, if he is the reason you can move on from what's-his-name, then good for you."

My phone lit up.

"It's him." I smiled with a mouth full of pot stickers.

Thedé cackled out loud. "Ha! Girl, calm down."

"Give me the keys to your car so I can talk to him."

Thedé slid them across the table. "Be cool."

Racing towards the exit I answered. The music and ambiance drowned him out until I reached the parking lot. Then, I faintly heard him say, "I called your house phone and didn't get an answer. Sounds like you're still partying."

"Not at all. I'm out to dinner with a friend."

"So you guys worked out your issues on the trip home?"

"No. Not those girls. My real friend who advised me not to go with the ones you met."

"But then we wouldn't have met. Gotta take the bitter with the sweet, Sweetness."

"True."

"You've been on my mind all day. When are you coming to see me? I miss your little sexy ass."

"I thought you were coming to see me?"

"Trust me. I'm sorting shit out to make time for you. I was hoping your schedule was more open than mine."

"I don't have any plans until the Fourth of July. Going to Clemson for my family reunion."

"That's a month away. I want to see you now."

"So whatchu gonna do about that?"

"Try to move some things around, but if I can't would you mind me crashing your family thing? I have a meeting in Atlanta the following week."

"Feels like our schedules line up best that weekend."

"That's not the only thing that feels right."

His words filled my stomach with butterflies. I re-entered the bar with a full chest and stroked ego, and could hear Thedé's laughter over the music and chatter as I walked towards her.

She raised her hand and slapped mine midair. "That's what I'm talking about! Look at you!" she said, loud enough for everyone sitting at Kandi's table to hear.

She rolled her eyes as Thedé continued.

"He kept his word so he gets another point from me, and this glow he's given you suits you." She clapped her hands." *What he say?*"

Chapter 6
Your Love Is King

He said it first. Those three confusing words a romantic like myself yearned to hear when they've become smitten with a love interest. Two insatiable nights of mind blowing sex, and a week of listening to each other take self-guided tours with finger play via telephone, Cade ended the call with, "I love you."

I believed he did because I felt the same, but was frazzled in my head with the do's and don'ts of how not to lose a guy's interest. And saying I love you prematurely was at the top of that list. But I said it back.

Simple love letters arriving at my door romanced me, then one arrived with my special request of a photograph. I needed it to refresh the image of him in my head. It also came in handy during our steamy conversations, and whenever the need to double click the throbbing aches struck me from the mere thought of him.

Distance was making my heart grow fonder. The stranger I had fallen in love with was easy to talk to, and our conversations never lulled as he was forthcoming in our discussions of music and sports, our work, dreams, and families. And with the love word now shared between us, I trusted we had something special.

"Being an only child, I want a boat load of kids," he shared.

"I'm just the opposite."

"You don't want children?" He sounded shocked.

"Maybe one– way off in the future, but it's not on my list of things to do at the moment. Does that make you cancel me out?"

"Nope. I know I can make you change your mind."

I laughed out loud. "Good luck with that."

He lowered his voice to a provocative tone. "You wouldn't give me a baby one day?"

"So you think talking to me in a sexy voice is going to change my mind?"

"It's working, isn't it?"

I lightly scoffed. "I can tell you're smiling."

"You didn't say no, so that's a yes."

When he talked like that I melted on the inside. It erased any doubts circling in my head that I was being duped, and convinced me his words and actions were genuine.

A routine slowly formed where the bulk of our conversations were overnight when he ran his warehouse. No matter the hour, I answered his call, addicted to the sound of his voice.

"Your voice gives me an eargasm. You know that?"

"I know I miss you and would like to be inside that wet pussy you got me beating off to every night."

"Well you have my address."

"I was hoping you missed me enough to meet me in Richmond for a night?"

"If my car could make it that far, I'd be there in a heartbeat. The Honda is good for getting me around locally, not long distance."

He huffed at my response, but I held my ground. He needed to make his way to see me. The Queens who raised me taught me early on, a man will come to you when he wants you. The rules of the game state, you don't run behind a man when you have the pussy. Pussy is power, and a man will work for it...Pay for it... Even slay for it. It makes the world go 'round, caused wars in mythology, makes and breaks marriages, creates and delivers life, and is desired every second of every day. And the words my mother spoke held weight.

"What the fuck you look like holding that much power between your legs and running behind a man? He'll come to you if you are what he wants."

Since I'd easily given myself to Cade, I needed him to prove he wasn't just bumping his gums with enticing words. He needed to prove how much he desired me, and show me his profession of love was real.

"What if I send you money for a rental? I gotta see you, Sweetness," he begged.

"You will in ten days."

"God, that seems like forever," he whined. "Ten more days of a relationship with my right hand is how you're gonna do me."

"You come straight out of a comic book." I laughed.

"I showed my drivers the picture you sent me. Whew." He paused. "I damn near rubbed the skin off my dick looking at it. That red hair suits you. Keep it like that for me."

"You like that, huh?"

"You're gonna find out when I see you."

As I blushed and yearned for that day to arrive, and imagined what we would say to each other once we were face to face, a loud voice shouted in the background.

"Who you over here talking to, bwoi!"

"Come on, man." Cade muffled the voice by placing the phone to his chest.

"Over here all huddled up in the corner making love to the phone. They talking about you on the floor," the guy carried on. "What she look like?"

"You already know what she looks like."

"Oooh. That's shawty with the red hair?"

"Yeah, man. Go away."

"She got any friends, sisters, aunts?"

"Baby, I gotta go. This fool ain't gon' let up. I need to get back to work anyway. You going to sleep, or you want me to call you back?"

"Call me back. I want to finish this conversation."

Cade whispered into the phone, "So do I. Go ahead and take your panties off and start without me."

I was all in, accustomed to the verbal savagery, content with pleasuring myself to the sound of his sensual voice filling the void of loneliness.

He rang hours later. "Aw man. You fell asleep on me. I can hear it in your voice."

"I did. What time is it?"

"Five o'clock. Two more hours, then I'm headed home to dream of you."

"Why is it quiet?"

"I'm sitting in my car. I think my partner knew what I was doing the last time." He chuckled. "You ready for me?"

"I did what you asked."

"Prove it. Let me hear you slap it. And tell me everything you're doing."

My walls throbbed as I placed the phone on speaker, then slid it above the stubble prickling near the line of my center.

"I'm parting my sea with two fingers, opening my pussy..."

"Whose pussy?"

"I mean your pussy... wide open. Cold air from the AC is blowing directly on me."

"How does that feel?"

"Cool. Stimulating."

"Warm my pussy up, baby."

"My index and middle fingers are hovering above it."

Tap. Tap.

"Oooh. I hear you smacking it. Tap that pussy, Sweetness."

I tapped my exterior in a random rhythm. *Tap. Tap.* With one finger. *Pat. Pat.* With two fingers. *P-p-p-p-pat.* I sped up the slaps and grunted from the sensation.

"Baby, I'm harder than a brick mason laying foundation."

The sides of my mouth turned wet as I sighed. "That's what you need to be sending me pictures of," I said, laying the phone between my breasts.

"Humph. I just might. Now put those same fingers in your mouth and let me hear how you'd suck my dick."

"I don't do that."

"You will."

I gulped at his authority. Below the covers suddenly turned hot and heat formed a dewy sensation across my body.

"You there?" He breathed heavily into the phone.

"I'm here."

"So, what you waiting on?"

I let out a deep exhale and placed two clean fingers in my mouth. Humming, I licked them and smacked on the saliva slipping between the cracks.

"Slurp, baby," he whispered with joy in his voice.

I had never done such a thing in my past, but there I was in the darkness of my room, releasing inhibitions and obeying his command. My tongue wrapped around my fingers, as my lips produced sucking noises to his pleasure.

"I can picture those pretty lips of yours like you're right in front of me. Tell me what you taste like?"

I paused. "You know what I taste like."

"I damn sure do. Slap that pussy again."

I moved the phone closer to my southern lips. *Pat, pat.* "Like that?"

"Again."

Pat. Pat. Slap.

"I know that pussy wet as fuck. Come for me."

Cade sighed heavily as I moaned on my end, rubbing my clit, and squeezing my legs tighter than a coiled snake wrapped around a tree.

"Talk to me." His raspy voice pleaded. "Paint me a picture, baby."

"I...I...can't."

"Tell me how you're rubbing my pussy."

"Hard."

"How many fingers?"

"Two." I panted.

"You sound close. Wish I was there watching you right now."

His lips sounded like they were pressed to the phone. The hunger in his groans encouraged my fingers to increase the speed of friction against my nub. I rubbed it in a circular motion and my shoulders felt a sizzle.

My arms locked near my chest. "Unh," I respired, then held my breath.

A surge exploded in my chest as my yoni pulsed.

"That pussy throbbing for me, baby?"

"Yes." I sighed.

Quietly he came with a mild holler, cursing at the jizz spitting on the steering wheel. "I'm gonna have to bring towels to work." I could hear him searching the compartments for napkins. "This might not have been a good idea," he said.

"Why not?"

"Cause now I'm tired as hell and gotta get this last load out of here in less than two hours."

"I'm sorry."

"Don't be. I might be tired as hell, but I'll get this shit done with a smile on my face. You get some rest."

"I will."

"J.C., I love you, girl."

"I love you, too."

Chapter 7
Lovers Rock

He kept his word.

"Just got off the exit. You mind talking to me for the rest of the way?"

I stepped outside to the porch with my insides frittering into tiny particles. I felt light as air as if I had wings formed on my back carrying my body afloat like Mary Poppins in my mother's front yard.

"Of course I don't mind," I said with a shaky breath.

"What's up with your voice?"

I could tell he was smiling from the way his tone lifted. "I'm a little nervous. It's the moment of truth."

"Oh shit. You didn't think I was coming."

I neither confirmed nor denied his assumption. A part of me believed he would show, the other part protected my pride, and my heart, by preparing myself for a letdown with an excuse of why he couldn't make it after the weekend had passed.

I lied to him. "By moment of truth, I meant I am overly excited we are finally going to be face to face."

"I know what you mean. This has been the longest month." He sighed. "I'm turning on your mother's street. The wait is over."

Giddy would be an understatement of how I shrieked silently, and beamed with enough happiness to spread throughout the neighborhood.

'The man came to get what he wanted. Me.'

A truck slowed down and turned on the rock path in my mother's yard. My brothers and their friends stopped politicking under the shade tree, turning their heads towards Cade parking his Virginia tags. Not one beer can touched a mouth.

"Playboy, you lost?" Cleve, the eldest of our quad, yelled across the yard.

"Nah." Cade looked at me. "I'm at the right house."

I stepped off the porch. "He's here for me."

Norrie, the second born, chimed in. "Here for what? To get his ass beat?"

"Don't start," I warned.

Cade walked towards the porch and chills froze my back. He smiled at me from across the lawn and my cheeks turned redder than my hair. He appeared to be walking in slow motion as I stared at him with a fluttering heart and goosebumps prickled on my arms in the sweltering heat, so I met him halfway on the sidewalk in front of the sunflower patch and sprouts lined up in the dirt on each side of the stone.

"I kept the red hair, like you asked."

He leaned down, gripped my waistline, kissed me, then whispered. "I'm ready to go mess it up."

"You're smart not to say that out loud in front of my brothers. They really will whip your ass." I snickered, wrapping my arms around him.

He exhaled. "This feels exactly how I imagined it." Then pulled away. "My dick is getting hard."

"Yes it is." I pinched his cheeks. "Let me introduce you to everybody, then sneak off for a bit."

My brothers approached with intimidating stares at Cade. I

placed my hand in his, and gazed back at them with lasers in my eyes.

Cleve led their planned agenda. "You got a lotta nerve kissing on my little sister. Who are you supposed to be?"

"What's up, I'm Cade." He stretched a balled fist forward.

My brothers laughed.

Norrie looked at him from head to toe. "I don't like the looks of him. I definitely don't like you touching on my little sister." He focused on our hands intertwined.

"Little sister? I am a grown woman." I sucked my teeth.

Norrie scoffed. "You just got grown, Jaya."

"My bad, man." Cade unlocked our fingers. "I didn't mean no disrespect."

"Your tag says Virginia. You drove all the way down here to see my sister?" Cleve asked.

"I did."

"For what?" Norrie interrogated him.

Cade swallowed big. "Huh?"

"That's a long way to 'just' come see somebody." Norrie narrowed his eyes at Cade.

"He came down for the reunion," I added.

"Is that right?" Cleve grinned. "You came to meet the family?"

"I hope that's cool?" Cade looked down at me and smiled.

"We'll see," said Norrie. "Let's take this to the back and get him liquored up."

"Ugh, no." I grabbed Cade's arm. "I have to show him how to get to the hotel after he meets Mama."

"What? Is the hotel gonna pick up and move or something?" Norrie laughed, waving his hands at their friends sitting under the tree to follow him. "It'll be there."

I rolled my eyes at him and walked Cade inside. Ma welcomed him into her home, staring at him more than she spoke. Then, Wild Bill strolled through the door.

"Who is this pretty motherfucker?" asked Shawnnie, my big sister.

"You and that mouth." My mother huffed. "This is your sister's friend, Cade. He traveled all the way down from Virginia to see her."

Shawnnie looked him up and down. "Is he coming to the reunion?"

"He is." I smirked.

She laughed out loud. "Cousin Man and Butterball are gonna tear him up. Do you see how pretty this motherfucker is? Have Cleve and Norrie seen this guy?"

I sighed. "They have already started in on him. They don't need you to pile on."

Shawnnie hooted and hollered making her way through the living room with an armful of bags in tow. "This is gon' be good. Where are Cleve and Norrie now?"

"Out back," Ma said.

She looked back at Cade. "It was nice meeting you. Don't pay us no mind. We good people."

Ma shook her head and hurried Shawnnie off with the wave of her hand. "Some of my children are...like Jaya here. The rest– just ignore them."

Shawnnie ran back and kissed Ma's cheek, then aimed for the back door. As it crept open she yelled, "J.C.! Stop smiling all goofy!"

I held my head down and blushed. "Mama, I need to show him how to get to the hotel. We'll be right back."

"Umm huh. It was nice of you to come down, young man."

I grabbed my purse and rushed Cade out of the door. We rolled out of the yard and sped to the hotel with his hand on my thigh, kissing at every red light. I stared at him as he drove, admiring the sexy way he turned the wheel of his truck with his lower palm, remembering how his eyes glistened in the bright sun on the beach.

His teeth sank into his full lips when he looked at me at the final red light. "Why you so sexy?"

"I get it from my mama." I laughed.

"Yeah, you do. Moms is fine as hell."

I punched his arm. "Ahite now. Don't come down here and leave with blue balls."

He parked under the carport of the hotel. "Girl, don't even play like that, as bad as I have been jonzing for you."

He hopped out of the car and little things I didn't have time to notice when we met stood out to me. How fast he walked, how thick his neck was, and how tiny his ears were compared to the size of his head.

'Definitely a footballer.'

All I saw when we met were his pretty whiter than white teeth, kissable full lips, whiskey coated eyes, and a cocky chest. I even overlooked the fact that he wore jewelry. The only man I would accept wearing a big ass gold chain is Nasir Jones.

'So where was this big ass necklace with the humongous gold and diamond cross when I met him?' I wondered.

I convinced myself that it was my nervousness trying to find something wrong with him. And my family picking him apart like a new kid on the block wearing Skippys didn't help either.

He came back to the car and wheeled it near the back of the hotel near the pool. My heart pumped like I had been running a race when he leaned over and kissed me gently on the lips.

"We're on the first floor. You ready to go in?"

"After you." I studied him up close below the moon roof.

"Why are you looking at me like I'm some science project?"

"Am I that obvious?"

"Yeah." His voice fractured. "Everything alright?"

I nodded." I'm just taking all of you in."

"And?"

"And I was thinking how we are spending time together at yet another hotel."

"So you're having second thoughts?"

"Hell no. You better take me inside and do all those things you said you were gonna do to me."

Cade looked down at his zipper, then back at me. "I hope we don't have neighbors."

Up went my legs, climbing him like a tree and wrapping around his waist before he dropped his bags. "I fucking missed you, Sweetness." He moaned in my mouth, kissing me and stealing my oxygen with the passion of a soldier coming home from war.

I sighed between his lips, losing patience to feel him inside of me. The dreams of him thrusting against me had come true, playing out differently than they had in my head. I envisioned we would have jumped bones on sight and played catch up during pillow talk. But this way was just as mesmerizing as he was now tangible and present to take me as his prey.

He carried me past the first bed and stopped in front of the mirror.

"Look at us. We look good together. Don't we?"

"Don't let my sister hear you talk like that." I squealed with laughter.

He kissed my cheek still staring at our reflection. A light chuckle left my mouth as he spun me around, then turned back towards the mirror kissing me from the side of his mouth.

"I should have brought my camera to record this."

Sloppy kisses swapped between us as we vainly watched ourselves connect in real time like attention seeking whores in need of an audience to perform.

"I just might have agreed to that— with you."

"Definitely next time."

'Next time. Confirmation this isn't a one-time thing. Music to my ears.'

The back of my head pressed against the mirror and his lips wet my neck. My shirt lifted above my breasts, and the first nipple made its presence to the party. He toyed with it while I unbuttoned my shorts. The latch of my bra folded and pinched my back. Cade kissed the cushion of my breasts as his crafty fingers released my other nipple above my bra.

He mumbled, "Baby, are we still going raw? Please say yes."

"Yes." I foolishly agreed.

He exhaled joy with a grin on his face lowering to my waistline. My shorts fell to the floor with my panties stuck inside of them.

"Mmm," he moaned. "That's it. Open that pussy up for me, Sweetness."

Two fingers spread my folds for him.

He sniffed me again. "She is pretty as fuck. That picture you sent didn't do her justice." He touched my center, and I trembled. "And she's already dripping for me. I gotta taste her before I stab."

Rubbing his lips across my clit with licks, flicks, finger slicks and spit covering my slit, my shoulders wilted and my hips rolled forward. I held his crown as he worshiped me, and quickly came from the slurping sounds between my legs.

He took a breather and rubbed my hole with two fingers. "Can I come in you this time?"

I relished in the sensation my body desperately missed and thought to myself, *'Why do I tell this man yes to everything? Why does he weaken me so? And why do I get the feeling he knows I won't deny him full access to me?'*

I pulled him forward and froze when he entered, contemplating my answer. He released an, "Ah," then pulled his dick out to observe me. Our eyes gazed into each other's, and he placed himself back inside with more force this time, then pulled it back out after I gasped for air. "I remembered you liked it when I did that last time," he whined. Again, he plunged between my legs and swirled his cock around. "Fuck, girl." He pulled back out.

I was blazing hot by the look in his burning, bourbon eyes enjoying my tenderness. The tension he built between us from a simple touch mesmerized me into oblivion each time his head pierced between my orifice. Heat ran through my entire body as he teased me, working my yoni until she jumped with my thoughts high above the heavens.

He plowed back inside, and my pussy gripped his dick. My walls held onto him so tight he couldn't maneuver about without vigorous manipulation. And I lived for that stimulation. A dick more golden than the color of his eyes. A dick so good I yearned to be beaten by it. Controlled by it. Owned by it.

Strong and hard he thrusted forward to free himself. "I love when she bites me like that. That pretty pussy got some grip." He grinned. "I could play in it all day."

"How about all night?"

"Team no sleep it is."

I tasted my drip on his lips, kissing him with my eyes open. Below his lids I watched his eyes roll up and down, then observed his parted lips quiver with every deep punch until his teeth hid his bottom lip.

A catch in his throat stalled his breathing. "You trying to make me look bad, girl. Like I ain't got stamina."

"Stop holding that shit back."

"I'm fighting myself not to bust, but this tight ass pussy 'bout to win."

Both of my knees bent and pressed into my chest. Cade's hands cuffed the back of my thighs, and his pipe glued itself inside me. With the top of his thighs clung to my ass cheeks hanging off of the dresser, he hollered.

"Ooooh!" His short nails dug into my legs.

I rubbed the top of his head. "You get it all out?"

He lifted his torso. "Yeah, but I ain't ready to see how much.

I'm stayin' in your world for a little while." His head fell to my chest.

My hands strolled from his head, down to his back. I drew circles in the center of his spine, listening to him catch his breath.

He pulled out, and his crème trickled out of my hole. "That's a sight right there." He rubbed his seeds around my bush. "I'm gonna be mad about leaving that camera all weekend."

Chapter 8
Flow

Shawnnie had zero couth in any situation. She peeped Cade had changed his shirt when we returned, and called him out in front of Cleve and Norrie. I cut her with my eyes, seething below my teeth as she snickered holding a losing hand from where I stood.

Norrie gave Cade an identical look, chewing a toothpick on the side of his mouth.

I bent over and whispered in Shawnnie's ear, "Like you wouldn't change clothes after traveling all day." Then I nudged her head. "Stop trying to be funny."

She pulled me back down with a tug to my shirt. "You know you can't lie worth a damn," she muttered. "I know what just got fucked looks like, Goofy."

"You don't need to hold her hand so tight, bruh," Norrie complained.

With flushed cheeks Cade sighed.

"Thought we agreed that hotel wasn't gonna pick up and move?"

"And I thought I told you I was grown, and it's clear you're not because you would know how reservations work," I said.

"Well if it got canceled we would have made room for the playboy. How else we gonna get to know him?" Cleve sipped from his beer can.

"He's not a playboy. Show him some respect."

Cade grinned. "Babe, it's cool. Your brothers are alright."

"You don't know these fools like I do."

"Give the boy a beer and cut the cord." Cleve folded his hand and nodded to Norrie. "Deal him in."

Cade took Shawnnie's spot at the table. I stood behind him for a few minutes and observed the menacing faces of my brothers and their friends, then let the men be men.

The gossiping about me in the kitchen fell silent when I walked inside. Ma, who has never been good at pretending, looked over at Shawnnie giggling peeling potatoes.

"You've been all smiles since that young man showed up."

"Ma, stop following up Shawnnie. Please?"

She chuckled lightly. "I got my own two eyes. You love that boy."

"Oh my God. Stop." I sprinted out of the kitchen.

Shawnnie tossed a pecan shell at my back. I picked it up and threw it back at her, then raced to our old bedroom and locked myself inside.

Stretched across the bed I squeezed my hands between my thighs. The remaining seeds of Cade soaked through my panties while I held myself as the replay of our quickie occupied my mind. As I squirmed and tightened my thigh muscles, my cousin Spencer called and ruined my moment.

"Me and Porsha are on our way over there, cous. Heard you got some pretty boy down here in my aunt's house."

"Don't come over here following up my brother's nonsense."

Spencer cackled out loud on his end. "Norrie don't like this dude. Can't have any old rudy poo wanksta getting at my cousin."

"Whatever." I sighed.

"Y'all should come out to the club with us tonight."

"Who is us?"

"The usual suspects. You know everybody is home this weekend. Shit should be hot."

"I'm sure he's down. We'll come."

"Ahite bet. Be there in a sec."

"Give me a few minutes to come outside. I'm gonna get ready now."

While fumbling through my suitcase, Shawnnie knocked on the door.

"I need to get in there. Are you done playing with yourself?"

"Ha ha!" I sprung from the bed and wrapped my towel around my chest.

"Took you long enough." She barged in as soon as I unlocked the door. "You do remember this is our room?"

"You never get tired, do you?"

"Of what? Keeping you on your toes? Nevah." She tapped her shoulder with mine.

She paced around the room as if it were hers alone. Grinning like the Grinch, she studied me. Watching my every move to find something to pick at, or pick a part.

"I'll be out of your hair," I said, stuffing my products into my luggage.

Shawnnie snickered as I zipped my bag. "You must want Ma to cuss yo ass out. You know she wants you to stay here this weekend."

"Yeah, but she ain't letting Cade stay here."

"So. He's a grown man. He can spend the night at the hotel and be here for breakfast in the morning."

"Shawnnie, don't act like you don't spend the night in hotels through the week when I'm not home. Stop frontin' like you some kind of saint."

"Never said I was. I'm simply pointing out you can't do the shit I do."

"Well, looks like I am this weekend."

"And Ma is gonna poison him to everyone at the reunion tomorrow."

I sighed. "If you've said what you came in here to say you can go now."

She twisted the knob on the door. "One more thing. Next time you sneak off for a quickie, try not to make it so obvious. Hold his shirt up so he won't have to hide he's been digging yo hot ass out." She snickered. "Like two sex deprived hyenas who couldn't wait a few more hours to bump pelvises." She kissed her teeth and shook her head. "You truly are the entertainer of the family."

I unwrapped my towel and threw it at Shawnnie as she sauntered out of the room. She was successful in what she set out to do. Get under my skin.

After cooling off, I collected myself and floated outside in a bright, red sundress and matching strappy sandals. Cade smiled at me as he and my family were getting on well.

Spencer's girlfriend, Porsha, met me at the door and whisked me away to the empty side of the patio.

She tossed her hair and looked back at the fellas. "Where did you get him from?"

"The beach."

"Bike week?"

I nodded.

"And now he's here? That is unheard of."

"Picture it. A hot, summer holiday weekend on Myrtle Beach where black bikers travel from all over the world to horde the streets and be whores, but fate found us instead, pairing two lonely, horny strangers wandering the coast."

Porsha laughed. "Tell me you don't talk like that in front of him?"

I chuckled with her. "Not yet."

"He likes you."

"What makes you say that?"

"I saw how he looked at you when you came outside."

The heat in my cheeks flushed, matching my hair and my dress.

"And you like him a lot, too."

"We've already said I love you."

"Already?" She looked back at him once more. "Well, he might mean it since he came all this way for you."

"He seems genuine." I fell into Porsha, then covered my face. "We already snuck one in since he's gotten here."

"My Lawd. And he ain't made up no excuse to leave with you throwing it around like free milk? We might have a winner. Rule number one. Don't ever let him see your angry side."

"Why not?"

She scoffed. "I should have recorded you when you lost it over the last bum you brought home. It is not becoming and you will run him off faster than a white woman's tears when they're in the wrong."

"Yeah, I don't wanna do that."

"Just be cool. Stay calm. And breathe."

I let out a deep breath.

"And rule number two– Don't let him know how much you like him. This might be the one."

Chapter 9
Somebody Already Broke My Heart

Before I could tell Porsha her words of advice were a day late and a dollar short, Cade interrupted us.

He draped his arm around me and kissed my cheek. "Lady in red. You looking fire tonight. I take it your cousin told you he wants us to meet him at some club?"

"Yeah." I pointed to Porsha. "We were just talking about that."

"Are you ready to leave so I can get fresh then?"

Porsha tiptoed towards the table. "Call me when y'all are on your way."

"Will do," I said, with enlarged eyes as my breath hitched.

"What was that about?" Cade asked.

I paused, searching for the right words. "Don't mind me. I let my sister get in my head. We ought to tell my mother we're leaving, I guess."

"What did your sister say?"

I blushed. "In a nutshell, she's made me nervous about walking past my mother with a sleep out bag."

Cade chuckled. "You can sleep in one of my t-shirts. Won't be the first time."

As Cade showered, I paced around the hotel room bombarded with everything thrown at me the past few hours. Shawnnie's taunts, Norrie's disdain, and Porsha's advice.

'How bad is my temper?' I wondered.

There were a few instances where I went off the deep end, but as Ma put it– My reactions to people's actions needed work. Those reactions were also why things ended with my previous boyfriend in a tumultuous manner, let her tell it without any knowledge of the truth.

All she knew was I didn't act like the lady she raised me to be. But to this day, I will stand by my choice of swinging at him with a baseball bat when I learned my suspicions of him cheating were indeed true, with not only one, but two girls, and one of them had been carrying his baby for five months.

Thinking about the way he burned me resurfaced the hostility I felt the night Porsha saw me lose my cool. The night she apparently couldn't forget. The night it took her interference to snap me back into reality.

Some loud mouth girls that lived across town and attended our rival school, showed up to a football game claiming they had been hooking up with our boyfriends. The boldest of them all stood in front of my high school sweetheart while we were snuggled in each other's arms.

"How'd you sleep after we hung up last night?" she asked him.

"I don't know what you talking about. I was on the phone with my girl right here." He squeezed me tighter.

I pointed at the girl. "I'm not the one to do a lot of talking. That's the only warning you'll get."

"Well your boyfriend sure does a lot of talking when you go to sleep."

I had no choice but to show my ass. I pulled out a switchblade and chased that bitch until her track star ass put a huge dent between us. Sure a couple of obscenities flew from my mouth and I threatened to bloody her body and throw her in the woods to feed the animals, but it was in the heat of the moment.

Wasn't I justified?

Then, just last Christmas I brought home a fool I wasted a year dating. His pathological lies didn't go over well with my family who are quick to call you out on your bullshit. To save him from the hole he was digging further into the ground, we met Spencer, Porsha, Butterball, and a few of my other cousins at the same club Cade and I were off to.

Just like every holiday, the club was packed with alumni from all around, but I didn't pay close attention to who was present until it was too late. The same reckless mouth girl from high school was showing too many teeth in my fool's face. The fool who made a horrible impression with ridiculous lies to sell himself as something he was clearly not. The fool who only presented a false side of himself to me. The fool who was easily swayed into taking shots with a random woman who had a personal vendetta towards me.

I slipped between them at the bar. "You put doubt in my head with the other one. Is that your goal here tonight, too?"

"Oh, he's with you? I didn't know." She lied.

"I think you did know. I don't believe in coincidences. Especially coming from you. So, what's your deal? Stalker much? Obsessed much? Help me understand why you want to be in my shoes so badly?"

"My feet would never walk in those."

"You're right. Clown feet belong in clown shoes." I turned to my ex-boyfriend. "And as for you, I hope she lets you stay at her place tonight and drives you back to Fayetteville. She stalks me so I'm sure she knows where I live. Your shit will be on the porch."

"Jaya!" He pulled on my arm.

My cousins surrounded him.

"I was just having a drink with this girl."

The vibrato in his voice was his tell, and I could feel the lie crushing my bones. I had watched them flirt for at least five minutes and two songs, and nothing about that drink, or their conversation was innocent. He fell for whatever game she was playing, and the doubt seed already planted inside of me from the lies he spat at my mother's house had blossomed into a full stinking rose.

Any doubts I had about him over the past year, any story he had corroborated that never sat right with me, and all the times he was late for our dates came rushing back.

Porsha drove me home, and along the way I called friends of friends to help me track down one girl on campus I had a funny feeling about.

Porsha veered into the median. "Don't call that girl."

"All I need her to do is deny or confirm."

"Either or, this relationship is over. He's a liar. That girl is probably a liar, too. You'll never get the truth. Just say fuck it and move on. I'd rather you go back to the club and beat that bitch's ass."

"Why do you think she has it in for me?"

"I don't know. But this is her second time fucking with you, and twice is too many times for me."

"I don't want to fight over a man. Just take me home."

Porsha came inside and sat in the living room as I packed up the fool's things. He showed up to the house with Spencer and Butterball.

I threw his bags on the porch. "He is not staying here. Take him home with y'all."

Butterball laughed. "I'm out, cous. I don't approve of him no way."

"Jaya, be for real." My ex pleaded.

Porsha stepped outside. "Remember what I said."

"We'll sit out here and wait for a few minutes. Y'all work this out," said Spencer walking Porsha to her car.

"How you gonna bring me home and treat me like this?"

"Why did you come home with me knowing you're a big liar, and aren't serious about this relationship? You've embarrassed me in front of my family, and in the public. Spencer, take him to Greyhound."

"I can't believe you are mad about me having a drink at a bar."

"Answer this, how long have you been sleeping with Kami?"

"Man, that's old news." His voice vibrated.

I threw one of my mother's plants at him. "Get off of my porch!"

He ducked. "If that had of hit me, I swear I'll..."

"You don't want me to wake up these country boys 'round here. Get yo ass on the bus and be gone!"

Spencer pulled him off of the porch. "Come on, man. Off to the bus station you go. I can't let you square off on my cous, and I don't wanna fight you."

As he followed Spencer to the car, he yelled, "Kami ain't the one you need to worry about."

Instantly, I knew he meant my roommate. The roommate who was always quiet when I vented about my relationship. The roommate that never had anything to offer when I expressed my insecurities.

Darkness no longer surrounded me as I was fully lit with rage. I took my mother's hedge clippers and cut his bag open, slicing every piece of clothing he had packed in half. I tossed his toiletries into the road, and threw his shoes down a muddy trench where the water drained from the gutters on the side of the house.

He scrambled through the pile of sheared clothes looking for something to salvage. And while he shuffled through the mess, I ran to the backyard and returned with a baseball bat in my hand.

Spencer picked me up by my waist mid swing. "Calm down, cous. You can go to jail if you kill him with this!" He pried it from my fingers as I fell to the ground.

I jumped back up to my feet and eased over to the porch.

Norrie's hidden lighter under the brick on the bottom step twinkled at me in the moonlight. I flicked the wheel and smiled at the spark.

Porsha ran out of the car. "Un uh, J.C. Don't do that! You might set yo mama's yard on fire! He ain't worth the time! Spencer, put him in the car and let's go! Jaya, you go in the house!"

Cleve drove up as Spencer pushed my ex into the back seat. I let the flame die when he jumped out and ran towards Porsha with one foot in and one foot out of her car.

Cleve stretched his arms. "What's going on?"

"Everything is under control. Take yo sister in the house and clean this mess up before yo mama sees it. Jaya will tell you what happened."

"Is my sister alright?"

"She's mad as hell, but she's alright." Porsha tittered.

Cleve approached me on the sidewalk. "You care to tell me what's going on?"

"Not really. But I need you and Norrie to do me a favor."

"Anything."

"Follow me back to school after New Year's. I need you and Norrie to help me move in with my bandmate until I can find a place of my own off campus."

The shower turned off. "Penny for your thoughts," Cade said, standing behind me smelling like spring water from a mountain dripping wet in all of his glory. The sight of him threw the fiasco from Christmas to the back of my mind where it belonged. I swayed side to side, taking all of him in for the first time as every one of our encounters had happened too fast and in the dark.

Without his fisherman hat covering his beautiful face, I saw the golden eyes that ogled me on the sidewalk. The whiskey and golden brown skin dripping wet past his even darker and erect penile path. The bicep cuts in his arms. The lines below his chest pecs and the fading rips in his abs and robust thighs.

I stared at his chestnut erection. "That's for me, I suppose."

'*Mama was right. I am in love.*'

He brushed water beads from his hair with a towel then dried himself off, grinning at me watching him put on a private show for my eyes only. "While I was in the shower, I was thinking about you in that red dress, and this happened." He pointed to his cock. "It's up to you, but I wouldn't mind wrinkling your dress before we go out."

"If I wrinkle this dress, I'm not going out. If I take off this dress, I'm not going out. You get where I'm going with this?"

His head leaned to the side and he threw the towel to the floor. "Did I just hear you want to be punished for defiance later?"

'*The fuck is he talking about?*'

"This time, I'm going to make you wait for it." I sat on the other bed and crossed my legs. "Take me out and show me off."

"I can do that. If you give me a kiss first."

I eased into his arms.

He held me by the face and softly kissed my lips. "You smell good. You taste good. You look good. You feel good." He moaned between each peck.

I traced the dip below his smooth chest with my fingers on the edge of falling for his temptation. "So do you. Now get dressed."

Chapter 10
All About Our Lore

Cade didn't dance. Neither did Spencer. Gangsters mainly held up the walls at all events, and this is where we spent most of the night inside the club.

As my cousin predicted, the club was packed. A little too packed. And like most gangsters, that made Spencer uneasy. It was also the first time I noticed Cade didn't seem like himself. His eyes appeared shifty and beady-eyed at times as if he were paranoid. But as the music mixed and brought the crowd to life, he seemed to settle in, and I stopped babysitting him.

Porsha and I took to the dance floor. The beer sipping wall-flowers watched as men danced with the two of us, then sent Spencer's goons to break up our good time whenever the moves became too provocative.

Porsha and I laughed at their cock blocking. "You think Spencer is corrupting my man?" I asked her.

"I don't take him to follow someone else's lead. He fits right in with that bunch if you ask me. Did he tell you what he does for a living?"

"He's on the practice team for The Skins and owns some kind of tech supply communications company."

Porsha burst out into laughter. "Girl, that man hustles."

"No he doesn't. He calls me all night from his warehouse."

"I'm sure he does. Where he houses his product. Trust. That football slot pays for the cover. I know a hustler when I see one."

I glanced over at Cade standing in the corner. "Keep me posted on whatever Spencer finds out. They do look a little chummy."

Our eyes met and he waved for me to leave the dance floor. I sashayed my way over to him and planted a slow kiss on his lips in front of everyone.

His hand traveled down my back and he grabbed my ass with a firm hand. "You're having too much fun out there without me."

"I can get used to you being jealous. Come show me your moves."

"I'd rather dance with you in the room. How long do you want to stay out here?" His palm pressed the lower dip of my back, bringing me in closer.

"Maybe another hour so Porsha isn't the only girl hanging around my cousin and his gazillion hitmen."

"I'll be good and fucked up in an hour. You'll have to take us in."

"I can do that."

'Trusting me with the keys to his precious ride.'

I swooned.

To hide my telling expression, I turned around and danced against him. The racy movement of my body sliding back and forth on his manhood made his dick jolt. His hand brushed my stomach as he grinded on my ass, swaying with me to the beat.

To the left of us, Porsha and Spencer began to argue loud enough to cause a scene.

"Should we intervene?" Cade asked.

"Nah, it wouldn't be right if the two of them didn't have a spat, or slap each other."

"Slap each other?"

"Yes. That's a story for another time." I sighed. "The short version is my cousin has a wandering habit, philandering eye, and money in the bank. Bitches love that type of shit, and Porsha puts up with it for some reason. Money is nice, but not making me look like a fool is better in my opinion."

"Not once have you asked me for anything. I'd give you the world because of that."

I looked at him over my shoulder and smiled. "You really have a way with words, Mr. Williamson. And all I want is to be loved."

"And I love you." He kissed my temple. "You told me you were a singer. You left out dancer."

"You want to join me out there and see how good I am? Rumor is, a man who can dance has all the moves in the bedroom."

Cade choked as he laughed. "Nice try. I'm not coming out there with you." He squeezed my hips as we rocked side to side. "This is as much as you'll get out of me, until later on."

I reached back and placed my hand behind his neck, winding with him in unison. His dick pulsed between my ass and my yoni tightened.

"What you doing down there?" His fingers tugged on my dress.

"Preparing myself for you."

"J.C. Baby, it's time I hear you sing. Let's go."

I sent word to Porsha and Spencer by way of his entourage and followed Cade out of the club. He tossed me the keys. "I don't let just anybody drive my truck." His brow raised. I shrieked and jumped in the air from a pinch to my ass. "I'm being for real," he said as he opened the driver's door and lifted me on the seat.

I lured him in between my legs. "Trust me like I trust you," I said, then licked his lips.

He snatched off his hat and placed it in front of his chest. "You better stop playing, girl." He grinned, walking over to the passenger side.

Light taps to the music beat on my thigh as his fingers traveled higher and higher from every bump in the road. We drove five minutes if that before the desire imploding between us, and *So Anxious* playing on the radio could no longer be ignored.

I veered off the main road and lifted the hem of my dress to my hips.

Cade pulled me over to the passenger side. "You read my mind. Sit on this dick, girl."

We entered poundland on the side of a dark country road. Nonstop fucking at pre-dawn in front of an abandoned house– me on top, riding him like a jockey, and he my horse. The passion between us fogged the windows as my shrieks matched Ariana's impersonation of Mariah.

The alcohol hardened and endured him longer than I anticipated, forcing me to work harder than I planned to feel the warmth of his exertion inside my walls. Cade smacked my ass hard, then followed with little pats to soothe my cheeks as I stroked his pipe vigorously, saddled across his thighs with the energy of the rising sun fueling me.

"You look pretty as fuck riding me, Sweetness." He sucked on my neck. "Exactly how I imagined you would. Take that shit."

I moaned as the sun rays burst in the backdrop of the sky with Cade's grip on my ass sealing my pussy around his dick. I could feel my performative work completing the pleasure contract we signed when the swelling of his tip, the tightening of his legs, and the firm hold he had on my hips locked me on top of him.

I clutched my hands around his neck and cut off his oxygen for a split second, grunting from the tense hold of his hands pressing me down forcibly against him. He sighed out of breath with his eyes closed and tilted his head back, filling me with a warm load. I was bound to his lifeline so taut, a jackhammer couldn't lift me. It was where he wanted me to be. Where he needed me to be. And where I enjoyed being, giving him the ultimate satisfaction of releasing freely inside my walls, irresponsibly, flesh on flesh.

I clenched my drip around Cade's barrel until it was empty. He exhaled a sharp sigh, then I rested my head on his shoulder. He pulled my head back from the nape of my hairline and stared into my eyes, groaning while catching his breath.

"You driving me crazy, Jaya Chanelle Marcel." His hands massaged my bum.

"How was that?" I sighed.

"Fucking fantastical." He humored himself.

I spun over to the driver seat and started the truck. "I rather enjoyed that myself."

"Choking me or fucking me?"

"Both."

He slept for the short drive back to the room and raised his head when the engine shut off. "We're here," I said, running my hand across his forehead.

"So you can handle my truck?"

"I think I've proven I can handle more than that."

His fingers squeezed my thigh. "Does that mean we're gonna fuck all night?"

I unlocked the doors. "I'mma let you rest up and get a second wind."

That didn't happen. Cade didn't catch a second wind until he fucked me a third time— Initiated from the munch meal he made of my aching pussy bravely withstanding the strength of his stabs. It was the punishment he promised in his letters of a hard, slow whine in the quiet of night with only my purrs and cries to fill the room. My pussy was sore, my clit swollen, and my heart full seeing how he couldn't get enough of me.

Knowing the feeling was mutual satisfied me wholly, but as the only person with a vagina in this relationship, I was thrilled to take a shower in the morning before he woke to avoid a fourth lashing.

I lied across the extra bed listening to him snore in his sleep equally as loud as the television. When he woke, he raised his head and narrowed his eyes.

"Two questions. Why are you over there? And did you go through my bag?"

"You pushed me out of the bed, so I showered and let you stretch out. And yes, I needed something to wear. I hope you don't mind. You didn't before."

"Come here."

I curled my lips and crawled back into the soiled bed with him.

"It's cool. Don't be nervous. What's on the agenda today?" He nestled me in his arms.

"Swing by my mother's house so I can change clothes, then spend an hour or two with my family is all I have planned."

"And after?"

"I wouldn't mind coming back here and relaxing for the rest of the night. We're both leaving out tomorrow so...how does that sound to you?"

"Like a plan."

Chapter 11
Immigrant

Coming from a long line of women who took to men with ease all the while living under the motto, *take no shit and leave no prisoners*, I looked forward to hearing what my aunt and cousins thought of my new beau. But when the men found out Cade played football, he was whisked away before they had a chance to feel him out.

Cleve's approval weighed with favor to my uncles. They took to Cade as if they knew him, huddled below the shade of the palmettos near the barbecue pit which raised a brow or two with the wise women sitting on the patio.

I expected my mother to berate me for spending the night out and missing breakfast. To my surprise, she spoke highly about Cade's good looks with her sister and cousins, then tossed in the subtle shade of his good manners while looking at me cross.

"And he said good morning when he came to the house even though it was noon." My mother smirked.

"He is a handsome young man," said my Aunt Wilhamena. "Too bad you met him at such a young age."

"What do you mean, too bad?" I asked her.

"Don't put your eggs in one basket with one good looking man when your life is just beginning. Surely, my sister taught you how to manage your boy toys. You're too young to be thinking about settling down."

I was stumped. I sat there without a rebuttal looking stupid and feeling exposed for falling in love. My mother's cousin, Babs, studied my reaction and smiled at me on the side of her mouth, then tapped my aunt on the leg.

"Wil, I think that ship has sailed. That chile is in love."

"I could have told y'all that with the way she was cheese eating the moment the boy pulled up to my house." My mother curled her lips.

Aunt Wil added more of her two cents into the chatter. "Well, if you don't talk some sense into my niece, I will."

"Look at her." My mother pointed her finger at me. "What sense can you teach a woman in love? We've all been there."

"That's my point. She hasn't lived yet. Who better to school her than the very ones who made mistakes first? Jaya, baby, this isn't the time to be falling in love. Have some fun. Live free as a bird in your twenties, then think about love and all the heartache it brings when you're thirty before your real estate loses value," said Aunt Wil.

"My Lawd, who hurt you, Auntie?" I snickered to myself.

"I hurt myself because I didn't know any better. Rule number one— Never take a man home from the club. Meet him in the club, and leave him in the club."

"I know that one."

"Rule number two— Waste his damn time. These men will use you and waste your youth. Do it to them before they do it to you. We heard about what happened with that fool you brought home for Christmas."

I huffed in my mother's direction.

"A pretty girl like you shouldn't be in a rush to miss out on what the world has to offer. Now for rule number three."

"How many rules are we gonna cover?" I mumbled.

Aunt Wil chuckled. "Three today. Three more next time, cuz it will be a next time. Mark my word. For the love of God, don't get pregnant."

I shrunk standing there and felt attacked from the amount of slips I had allowed Cade.

"Listen to Wil," Cousin Babs added. "With one exception."

"What's that?"

"If he's rich, get your money, honey."

Low chuckles escaped from every mouth on the porch—including Ma.

"Don't tell my chile no mess like that." Ma fanned her hands above her head. "And don't you bring no baby home you ain't planning on taking care of yourself. I've done my time."

Cousin Babs chimed in. "One more piece of advice. You should also know being pretty doesn't mean shit. All the babes of our day were cheated on with the ugly heauxs hanging down at the hole in the wall," she whispered, looking at Uncle Cole's girlfriend of twenty years from the corner of her eye. "Don't be like that one." She nudged her nose.

Aunt Wil added, "Asshole done dogged that poor gal out. Stole her youth, beat her when he feels like it, and she's still with him. I'll never understand it."

"I don't want to understand it. But you all don't have to worry about me. I'm in no rush to settle down yet, or have a baby." I looked into my mother's eyes. "Check back with me in a couple of years, though."

"Be free, chile. Travel. See the world. Meet gorgeous men in other countries. Go out with your girlfriends. Date however many men you please until you're 29. Then start running credit checks," said Aunt Wil.

I frowned. "Why credit checks?"

"Marry a man with bad credit, you'll live to regret it." She and Babs hi-fived.

"On that note, I better go check on my friend...Maybe inquire if he has a 750." I winked back at Aunt Wil.

I looked around the yard and couldn't set my eyes on Cade. The more I searched for him, I noticed Spencer was missing as well.

Porsha sat on the bench near the drink table in front of the pool house. Before I was within an earshot, she said, "I told Spencer to leave it alone, but you know he has a mind of his own, and you can't tell him shit."

My face quickly turned red.

She furrowed her eyebrows at me. "Didn't I tell you not to let that man see you angry?"

I grumbled. "Where did they go?"

"A question no woman will ever have the answer to."

I huffed. "Why would Cade go with him, though? And not say shit to me. I ain't his mama, but damn, can I get a little courtesy? Respect even?"

"I told you that man was a hustler. My money is on they went to meet the plug."

I was livid and didn't know who to be mad at the most. Spencer for being Spencer, or Cade for slipping off when we agreed we would only stay for a few hours, and taking off without any consideration for me.

The pit in my stomach twisted in knots with the worst scenarios playing in my mind. Either Porsha was right that they tiptoed out to meet the plug – which led to more questions of who was I involved with – or Spencer took him to tag team some bitches to prove a point that I couldn't trust him.

Neither scenario was ideal, and the longer they took to get back, the more I questioned his sneakiness, and my face turned redder than the flags waving in front of me.

Uncle Cole stumbled over. "Juke and Spencer ain't got back yet?"

"Who?" I asked with my voice raised to a falsetto.

"Juke. The young fella who plays ball. Your lil' boyfriend."

"He is on the practice team, and why are you calling him Juke? You don't know him like that."

"Sheeet. That boy says he's crazy about you. And he's getting us tickets. Don't fuck this up, baby girl."

I stormed off into the pool house with Porsha on my heels. She opened her mouth to lecture me about my red face and the smoke steaming from my ears. Then Shawnnie strolled in after us.

"That's not a good look, sis." She kissed her teeth.

"Tell me something I don't already know."

"You know them hens kept a close eye on your boy. All it took was for one of them to mention to Ma he left with Spencer, and now she's crossed with him."

"You sure it wasn't you? Or Norrie?"

"Believe it or not, no. We didn't have nothing to do with it." Shawnnie laughed. "Well, he had a good run for about eighteen hours. It's just as well. There's something shifty about his eyes."

"His eyes are gorgeous."

"And hiding something." She scoffed. "I don't care how cute he is. I don't like how wide he's got your nose open. Just be careful with him, J.C.– And I say that with love."

I believed her. Shawnnie gave me so much hell, it was easy to tell when she was being sincere. The elders, on the other hand, shook their heads at me when I walked past them to go inside of the main house for a private place to stew in my anger.

"He ain't in there," said my mother. "Hope Spencer don't get him in any trouble."

"My words are sounding pretty good now. Ain't they? Remember, I speak from years of experience, two ex-husbands, and three current boyfriends." Aunt Wil winked at me.

I escaped the heat, both physical and verbal, and sat alone in the den with a view of the front yard. Thirty minutes later,

Spencer's car turned down the dirt path, rolling slow with smoke seeping out of the windows.

I couldn't hide my disappointment. I always wore my heart on my sleeve, and my face always told someone how I felt about them. To save me from exploding, Porsha entered through the back door.

"Get that look off of your face before you fuck this up." She crossed her arms in front of her chest.

"I can't turn it off like that, and I ain't the one fucking up."

"It ain't nothing to be mad at. They came right back."

"Yeah, but from where? It don't take but five minutes for a quickie. Two if you good at it."

"Honey, the way he got you hoppin' around, I doubt that man got anything left in the tank to bust in another woman this weekend."

My red face turned blush and I laughed.

"Now straighten up."

I released a sharp exhale and stayed inside the house, while Porsha returned to the heat to chastise Spencer. It wouldn't be a family cookout if someone didn't show out, so in keeping up the tradition, the two of them did us the honors.

Shawnnie stepped inside with Cade on her heels. "Look who I found." She tapped him hard on his back. "Spencer got that good shit, don't he?" She cackled.

"Hell yeah." Cade laughed with her.

"You have fun?" My voice failed to hide my disdain.

He pulled me from the couch. "I'm having fun. Your family is cool people. Are y'all having something for Labor Day?"

"Why?"

"Planning ahead is all."

And just like that, my attitude vanished into thin air, and I was all in, overlooking the nonexistent apology, or explanation of where he snuck off to. A fool in love.

Chapter 12
Bullet Proof Soul

The night was quiet. Apprehensive and bittersweet. Leg to leg we laid in bed, sleeping in turns, missing the plot of a movie, and narrow eyed of exertion.

Mid-morning he gazed into my eyes and planted the most delicate of kisses on my lips. We remained silent in each other's arms still, carefully orchestrating what to say besides good-bye.

Packed before checkout time, cleansed, and spritzed with perfume and cologne, we stood in front of the bathroom mirror looking at one another's reflection.

Cade kissed my neck as both his hands wrapped around my waist. "J.C., I love you." His warm breath traveled down my back. "I was supposed to be on the road hours ago, but I'm finding it hard to leave you."

My heart fluttered as I held back tears. "I love you, too."

"You sure? You don't sound too certain."

"I can't shake the feeling that this is the last time I'm going to see you."

He kissed the other side of my neck. "We'll make this work."

"Seems impossible with training camp underway."

"I hope I see you before then."

"I'm leaving that up to you."

"I ain't letting you go, Sweetness. We didn't even make love this morning. You know what that tells me?"

"What?"

"It's not just about sex with us. You feel right lying next to me. You make me laugh and feel like a man. I won't lose you because of distance."

I believed him. Every word he uttered had me convinced I was special to him. His profession of love. The spiel of "We'll make this work." The speech about us being more than bedmates. And yet I didn't hear from him for two days until midnight when he was at the warehouse.

"Glad to know you made it home safe," I answered his call.

"I crashed when I got back, and all day yesterday."

"So your uncle said."

"He wants to meet you by the way. So, how did you make out? It was an eventful weekend."

I could hear him smiling on the line.

"I didn't get to rest much until now." My voice dragged. "I had a show, remember?"

He moaned as he chuckled. "And here I thought I wore out your vocal chords. The endurance of my baby is a true mystery. You are going to wear me out. And I like that shit."

"I know you do."

"Did your cousin tell you the plan for Labor Day?"

"Porsha did."

"You know I'll be in training, but we will spend time together."

"I know."

"Baby, I need to see you before then."

"What do you propose?"

"I want to buy you a car. Can we agree you need one?"

"What I don't need is a heavy bill, higher insurance, and a..."

"I'll take care of all of that. Let me do this for you. It is not going to hurt my pockets. I love you, girl."

"And buying me a car is your way of proving that?"

"I wanna see you. And you need it. Let me fly you up here, we'll go pick out a ride, spend a little time, then you can drive it back home."

"Eight weeks is a long time, but getting me a car isn't the answer."

"It's been two days and I already miss you like crazy."

"Let me look at the band's schedule and work some things out. As you said, we'll figure this out."

The offer of a new car excited me, but it was a bad idea, and not the answer to our problem. It was Cade's way of controlling me. To have me running up and down the road chasing after him whenever his schedule allowed, but a shiny, new toy wasn't enough to entice me to flip our roles.

After a few weeks of phone tag and failed attempts to reach Cade due to training camp, I started to reconsider his offer until he called me at an odd time.

"I have to be in Charlotte tomorrow, but I missed the turn in Petersburg and found myself cruising down 95. Imagine that."

I chuckled. "That's your story?"

"Hell of a coincidence. Don't you think?"

"I'll say."

Then, I heard a knock at the door. I squealed to myself as I ran to open it, and found light brown eyes glowing at me. A whiff of fresh mint and citrus buckled my knees.

"Do I need an invitation to come inside?" Cade grinned on one side of his mouth.

"You've never needed one."

I jumped in his arms, welcoming all of the passionate kisses he stored for me. His foot closed the door before he laid me on my sofa, filling the void of not feeling his touch for weeks.

The moans from his mouth aroused me to appease him however he wanted. Bent over the arm of the couch I received his first stroke. "Umph," he groaned, holding his cock to the top of my bare wall. "I missed you, Sweetness. Which way to the bedroom?" He stroked me twice. "Never mind. I don't think I'mma make it." His hips wound with deep, concentrated, fast jabs then he howled in delight. "One down," he whispered, pulled out, then turned me around to face him. "How's my favorite girl?"

Throughout the night I endured swirling thrusts, long kisses, nipple nibbles, intense eye fucks, and down under dining. His gaze held mine, connecting with me cosmically, transcending my psyche beyond borders of ecstasy.

Breathless, I laid on my bed, allowing my distant lover to have his way with me as he pleased. When and wherever he sucked, I shivered, completely entranced into his world, soaking my sheets like a river.

We fucked so hard we broke my headboard, landing lopsided in laughter finishing each other off. And nothing mattered in the world except the two of us, stuck together on the floor.

"These past weeks without you have been torture. We could do this more often if you would take me up on my offer." He gnawed on my cheeks. "We can go pick out something when the dealership opens before I need to hit the road."

"I'm still thinking about it. What if I give you an answer on Labor Day?"

He sighed. "I may have news about something in the works pretty soon. I don't want to jinx it, so I'm keeping quiet about it for now, but I'm going to be unavailable for a few weeks."

I sat up. "Unavailable how?"

"I mean we'll talk. Just not all night. And you'll need a car so we can be together when I have the time."

I stared at him with narrowed eyes.

"I'll tell you what's going on as soon as I know something." He assured me.

"And I'll give you my answer when I see you for Labor Day. I have news myself. The band has been booked in Richmond, Friday night before Labor Day, so we won't make it to the DMV until sometime Saturday."

"Who is we?"

"Me and Thedé. She travels with the band sometimes."

"I hope she doesn't mind spending her nights alone, cause once I get my hands on you, she's on her own."

Off he went to Charlotte. Leaving me with a broken headboard, cash, and the jokes of Thedé who stopped by to see it with her own eyes.

She tilted her head. "I'm happy, you're happy, and you get to experience shit like this."

I hugged Thedé from the side. "I am happy."

"That's clear. And at least you didn't put a hole in the wall and lose your deposit."

I lightly punched her arm. "Cade has that covered." I pulled out the wad of cash.

She scoffed. "You really are madly in love with this guy."

"This man has traveled to see me, met my folks, tells me he loves me, has offered to buy me a car, and wants me to come see him. The uncle who lives with him wants to meet me, who talks my head off when I call the house by the way, and he makes me feel good about myself. Why shouldn't I think this is serious?"

"Two words. Long distance. It doesn't work. You wanna know what else? You're twenty-two. I can go on. You've seen him a handful of times?"

"Who put you up to this? Shawnnie?"

Thedé giggled. "No. I haven't spoken with her, but I am now since we have something to talk about."

I rolled my eyes at her.

Thedé placed her hands on her hips. "Look, I came over to see this travesty, but also to ask you for a favor."

"Anything."

"Remember Scott, the guy I met doing deliveries at the hotel? Well, I decided to go out with him. He has a friend in town on business, and I need you to go on a double date with me tonight."

"No." I shook my head. "I just spent the past couple of hours buried beneath my man."

"You owe me."

"For what?"

"Shit, I don't know right off the top of my head, but I know you owe me for something. And besides, you don't want to hear the truth, but I'm going to say it anyway. Your man is fucking on something up in VA when he ain't fucking you, so at least keep yourself entertained."

"I don't like that, Thedé, but I'll go, for you. Just tell his friend not to expect anything."

***

Thedé came through with a prospect. Townes Wilson, an entrepreneur with his own trucking company, beautiful smile, and braids neatly cornrowed to the back like Eric B.

He came off a tad boujee at first, if men could be categorized as such, but as the evening went on it was clear I had misjudged him, mistaking his confidence for arrogance.

He wasn't my usual preference, but he was lovely to look at. Yellow skin with a slim build, dark brown hooded eyes, and a chiseled jawline that accented his strong features to perfection. And perfection was what he would be considered to most.

His gaze upon me at dinner kept me on edge. I felt like I was on the examination table in the doctor's office. His commanding presence forced me to act like a different version of myself. Like the version sitting in job interviews— Prim and proper with carefully thought word selections when answering his questions. And I didn't wolf down my food like I normally would. I pecked at a cobb salad most of the night while studying his tongue, seductively licking his plummy lips between bites of his food.

He and Scott both reached for the check.

"You did me a favor and asked Thedé to introduce me to her lovely friend here. Let me show off this time." He smiled at me.

"What if I reached for the check?" I asked.

A curve formed on the side of his lip. "Then I would ask **your** permission to let me show off this time."

"Good answer." I grinned.

The blush in my cheeks matched the backdrop of the restaurant. His style of flirtation was new to me. His brand of gentleman was new to me as well, and I found myself considering him. Enamored by him overall. His eloquent speech, worldly conversational skills, and satirical, charming humor captivated me, but the spark I yearned to feel about a man was missing. And when I laughed at his jokes, I felt guilty. Cade held that spark and was present even in his absence, clouding the potential of perhaps someone greater.

By the end of the night, Townes and I stood outside on the pergola, bonding over being thrown together by our friends.

"Tell the truth. Did you really ask to be introduced to someone, or were we the safety nets in case tonight didn't go well for them?"

He chortled. "Scott asked if I wanted to join him tonight so I wouldn't be bored at the hotel. I agreed, but only if he introduced me to someone interesting."

"So, you two have done this before?"

"What makes you ask that?"

"You don't strike me as the type who needs to be introduced to women."

"I don't know what you've heard, but the dating pool is just as slim for men as it is for women. At least I got lucky tonight."

"Lucky? How so?"

"Thedé brought you along. I haven't met a woman that makes me nervous in a while. You appear to be happy with life. You don't see that too often. Everyone is either faking like they are, or just fake all around lately. I don't get that vibe from you."

"I suppose I am happy."

"It's attractive."

Silence crept between us as he stared into my eyes. I glanced into his briefly, then looked away.

"I like it down here," he said. "If I were to open up an office around these parts, would you make time to see me?"

"That depends."

"On?"

"If I'm free."

"I sure hope you are. Here's my card. Call me anytime, day or night."

I tapped his card with my fingernail. "Whenever I choose, huh?"

"And I'll pick up. I mean it. Day or night."

When he said that I thought about Cade, and how I had more conversations with the uncle that lived with him whenever I dialed the house line, and how we predominantly spoke at night. I had spoken to him a handful of times when the sun was out, occasionally receiving a quick call between his training camp hours, and whenever he found time to sleep.

Then there was Townes Wilson. Tall, driven, successful, from a good family, well-mannered, respectful, handsome, and forthright, telling me he'd make time for me twenty-four seven. A catch in the eyes of many, including mine.

And I never called him.

Chapter 13
Cherish The Day

I couldn't wait to see him until Labor Day. I caved and hopped on an American flight out of FAY to DCA late one evening to feel the force of Cade overpowering me, smell the essence of his manliness wrapped around me, and see the words, "I love you," roll off of his full lips to empower my soul. Hearing them sent chills throughout my body, but seeing him say those sweet words while gazing into my eyes blossomed my heart tenfold.

My visit was short lived. Even shorter than his stay at my place. He picked me up at the terminal, and checked us into a hotel near the airport where the windows vibrated as the whirring crafts flew above and around us.

"You should stay another night. I'll give you some shopping money. You can go do as you like while I train, then I'll come by afterward and take you to dinner. And make that pretty ass bounce a few more times before you leave me again."

"I would if I could. My flight is already booked for 8 am. Labor Day is just around the corner. You'll have a whole weekend to make my ass bounce."

"Whose ass?"

"Shut up." I pinched him as I laughed.

"This feels nice. I wish you could spoil me every day like this."

"What if the distance is what makes this so great?"

"Fuck if I'mma believe that." Cade griped. "I want this every day. And when that day comes, it's gonna be all good."

"I can tell you miss me."

He squeezed me tighter so his lips could reach my forehead with ease. "Good. Because I do." His lips pressed my skin delicately. "I know how you can show me you missed me."

"I'm listening."

He rolled over onto his stomach and grunted. "Rub my back, baby. The field can be hell on your man."

Slowly I soothed his pain with a firm massage. He jumped when the sensation of my hands rolled around his tight shoulders. Then they slumped forward when I rubbed his blades in a circular motion.

"I'd be living the dream if I could wake up next to you rubbing on me like this."

"What do I get for being good with my hands?"

"Keep going. You'll see."

He moaned from the pressure of my fingers extracting the pain from his back. My knuckles kneaded his tense muscles until his dick grew hard, then he rolled over and lifted my thighs across his.

"I'm going to pay for this tomorrow, but I have to have you once more before you leave."

And he did. Twice.

I didn't see the city on that visit. Only the handsome face of my lover, the blush, linen covered walls that witnessed our debauchery, and a cloudless, dark blue sky upon my arrival, and when I departed.

But the sky wasn't as friendly when Thedé and I drove to the DMV from Richmond. Torrential rains threatened our travel heading north on the interstate.

"It's a sign. I swear it," she said.

"It'll pass." I fanned her off, putting an incoming call from Porsha on speaker. "Sup? Is it pouring down where you are?"

"Damn sky is black. A white party in this weather will have every hard nipple outside tonight playing peek-a-boo."

I snickered. "You sound excited."

Porsha joined in. "I've seen one or two fine ones roaming around the hotel. If your cousin acts up— sheeeeet, I might stand in the rain on purpose."

"He won't be having any of that." I tittered. "Have either of you seen Cade?"

"Not yet. How much longer 'til you get here?"

"With this traffic, maybe an hour."

"Well y'all be safe. See you then."

Thunder roared and lightning forced shrieks from Thedé and I as it lit the grey sky. Then, we dined with Porsha and Spencer after settling in at the five star restaurant on the atrium level.

"What's the plan for tonight, ladies?" Spencer yawned, rubbing his belly.

"If the weather clears, you can sit this one out." I exhaled a deep sigh.

"A ladies night sounds like fun since I'm fifth wheeling this weekend." Thedé added.

"The white party ain't really my speed, so cool wit' me." Spencer grinned. "Have you spoken to my boy?"

"Not since I checked in. Have you?"

"Earlier before his practice. I doubt if he wants to go to that shit either. Y'all go enjoy yourselves. If things change, we'll meet y'all out there. Just don't do nothing to make me have to lay a motherfucker on his back is all I'm saying."

Porsha rolled her eyes at him. "Let's get out of here."

One final check and we set off into the night. The drive started off quiet, dampening the mood like the roads.

I turned down the radio. "What aren't y'all saying?"

"That was too easy." Porsha huffed.

"Yeah, something ain't right." Thedé shook her head.

"They're up to something." Porsha agreed.

"They? As in my cousin and Cade?"

Porsha nodded with her teeth pressed into her bottom lip. "I can feel it in my bones."

"I knew this storm was a bad sign. Cade's ass should have been to the hotel to see you by now. Why wasn't he at dinner?"

I sighed. "He had practice today."

The two of them laughed.

"J.C., you got the pussy. That man would be jumping over buildings to see you if he wasn't getting none," said Thedé. "How long has it been?"

"Two weeks."

"How so?"

"He flew me up here for a night close to two weeks ago."

"Why you ain't say nothing?"

"It was a turnaround trip. I was gone for maybe twelve hours."

"Still." Porsha sucked her teeth. "I know something is up. Thedé, I'll be your wingman tonight 'cause this one's nose is too open to play."

Thedé and Porsha bumped fists.

"Bet that," said Thedé. "Don't judge me if I bring something back to keep me warm." She laughed.

But I wasn't laughing hours later haven't not heard from Cade, all the while turning down offers from beautiful black men glowing beneath the moonlight on the rooftop lounge. And the joke was on me by the time we returned to the hotel.

Chapter 11
Every Word

The fifth wheel turned out to be me. Thedé hung out with a random hook-up she pulled at the white party, and when the sun pushed the moon out of the sky, I found myself sitting alone in my room scanning texts and missed calls from Cade.

The embarrassment of it all confined me in my room.

"Open up." Thedé shouted from the hall.

"I'm good. Go eat without me. I'll order room service or something if I get hungry."

"You sure?"

"Positive. See you later."

Moments later after sulking and staring at my flaws in the long mirror, pulling on my cheekbones, and sucking in my stomach while questioning Cade's absence, a knock disrupted my downward spiral.

"I told you to go without me," I said, opening the door.

"You've told me no such thing," Cade said, with the left corner of his mouth curved upward.

"So you did remember I was in town?" I barricaded the door with my arm resting on the panel.

"Baby, I fell asleep before I hit the shower. When I woke up it was 4am. I called you. Are you going to leave me out here, or invite me in?"

"I haven't decided."

He placed one foot next to mine in the doorway. "You sure about that?"

"No."

He grinned and pushed me backward with his chest. "How about now?"

I didn't need to give him an answer, nor was I offered the opportunity. Cade lifted me in his arms, shut the door, and railed me against it. Between the housekeepers pushing their squeaky carts past the room, and Cade's vigorous grunts as he powerfully stroked me with a fistful of my hair forming a crick in my neck, I heard my very own thoughts express disappointment in the ease of which I gave myself away.

Post his exertion, Cade held onto me from behind. Delicate kisses aroused my neck as his fingers ran through my hair.

"Cade, what really kept you last night?"

He sighed, detaching himself from inside of me. "I planned on telling you tonight at dinner."

"Tell me now. I believe you owe me that much."

He zipped his pants. "You're right. I owe you more." He kissed my forehead. "It has to do with my being unavailable these past weeks. I'm in the 53."

"Meaning?"

"I've been promoted to the team. Second string."

I wasn't sure I had ever seen him smile so big. But there they were. Those bright, white, perfect teeth gracing me between his full, brown lips, and face overjoyed from his success.

"So you get to take the field?"

"It is likely."

"How exciting." I stroked his face. "I'm happy for you. And proud."

"Thank you, baby. I want to celebrate this win with you. I have a few hours until I'm due back for training. I know this isn't how we planned this weekend to go, but you know I'll make it up to you."

"Wait a minute. Are you blowing me off after you came here and scored a quickie?"

"No, I wouldn't do you like that. Grab your purse. I made reservations for us at one of my favorite spots."

"And then?"

"And then, I have a few more things I want you to see before I have to check in."

I sucked my teeth.

"Don't be like that. I'm coming back tonight once I'm done with everything. I promise."

I shook off my qualms and put on pretend happiness that our time together was scheduled in a micro window of time. The delicious french toast at brunch wasn't sweet enough to cure the sour taste in my mouth of my expectations not being met, all the while Porsha's face singing a tune in my head telling me not to show my angry side helped me keep my cool.

"What say we walk this meal off at the mall?"

"I didn't come up here to go shopping, Cade."

"It's not that kind of mall. You'll see."

The shame I felt walking along the manicured, green lawns of monuments, memorials, and museums was written on my face during the two mile stretch.

"When you said mall, I thought..."

Cade smiled. "Oh no. It's what they call it here."

"If you would have said you were taking me to the historic district I would have assumed you meant to see The Capitol Building and Lincoln Memorial and whatnot, but, I guess I learned something new. And obviously something I probably didn't pay attention to in high school." I snickered.

"Happy to see you remembered how to smile."

I looked up at him. "I'm just disappointed. I thought I would get to spend more time with you this weekend."

He took my hand and kissed the back of it. "We will. It may not be for months, but we will. Come on, time is getting away from me. I have two more stops planned for us."

One to two acres between each house down a country road outside of the city limits threw me for a loop. The grandeur I imagined his house would be, didn't come close to reality. A quiet neighborhood, one story home with vinyl siding, forest green shutters, two car garage with his truck, an old restored Ford classic, and his motorcycle covered in the corner, made me question where he had taken me. My gut said he didn't live there, but my mouth chose to be kind.

"Your house is nice."

"It's my starter home. With this promotion, I plan on moving us into something a little bigger."

Light taps on the wooden floors grew closer, then a crack of bones caught our attention.

"So we finally meet," said a shaky voice.

"Hi. I'm..."

"J.C." His uncle reached for my hand. "I recognize you from your picture. How you getting along?"

"Really good."

His uncle kissed the back of my hand with lingering lips.

Uneasiness caused my body to jolt. "Thanks for asking, and nice to finally put a face with the voice that keeps me company when this one isn't around." I leaned into Cade's arm.

"I don't mind at all. How long are you here for?" He sniffed my hand before I pulled it away.

"I'm leaving tomorrow."

"So soon? That's a shame." His eyes fixated on my breasts.

"Unc, we dropped by for a quick second. I'll be by after

training with dinner." Cade pressed his hand into my lower back and nudged me towards the front door.

"But you just got here?"

"I know, but my schedule is tight."

"You take care until next time." I waved and scurried out of the door.

Cade checked the time and his face appeared flustered. My pride pushed my anger to the side as I fastened my seatbelt.

"Just take me back to the hotel. I don't want to be the reason you are late."

"I think I can squeeze in the last place I want to take you."

The pit of my stomach churned when we said goodbye as the replay of our afternoon was nothing more than a quick drive by of the stadium, sightseeing, brunch in Tyson's Corner, and a quick introduction to his uncle that served as a distraction that I had come into town for a quickie and a handbag.

He lied to me. This I realized too late, after trusting all six foot two of him standing behind me, making promises he had no intention of keeping. The words, "Sweetness, I love you and I'll see you later tonight," rolled off of his tongue so persuasively, I didn't doubt him for a second.

The look of care and content on his face as I watched him kiss my neck and the back of my shoulder in the mirror convinced me he was my person, and that I had nothing to worry about. The promise in his honey-coated eyes made me a believer that time was our enemy, and we would defeat it. "The distance won't kill us. We'll make this work," he said. And I believed him. He had nothing to gain by telling me lies. He already owned my mind and helped himself to my body, and the love I felt for him was so deep, that lies weren't necessary.

Yet, I left the city of Washington embarrassed, outraged, and hurt, waiting for him to show up after practice. One hour late and not a word from him ruffled my feathers and shook my soul, and the rage I had been suppressing felt like explosives burning in my chest.

I convinced Thedé to leave in the dark of night with the determination to tackle the first shift on the road. Though my rage fueled me with the energy to drive us all the way.

"You deserve better, J.C. That's all I'mma say." Thedé hopped out of her car.

I hugged her and passed her the keys. "Thanks for using your car for my excursions this weekend. I owe you one."

"I mean what I said. I love you like a sister. And I don't like the look that asshole has put on your face."

"I don't want to talk about it. I'll call you tomorrow." I rolled my suitcase inside my apartment.

Cade called early in the morning, but I didn't answer. For days I ignored his call, wrestling with what to believe from his messages, and running repetitive questions in my head.

'Is he telling me the truth?
Does this new position require patience and understanding on my
part?
Was that his house or his uncle's house?
Am I playing the fool for love?
Is this how it ends for us?
What do I do with all of these feelings
I have for him?'

Chapter 15
Smooth Operator

By the weekend, roses covered my doorstep alongside a letter with a picture of him in uniform on the field.

I need you. I miss you. I love you.
Here's an open ticket.
Use it when you're ready.
Fingers crossed it'll be soon.
Your name will be at Will Call for every game.
I hope I see you in the stands.

Love, Cade

I didn't bite. I wanted to, but being easy going with him was causing me internal strife. Not what one desires to feel when in love.

Then, Sunday morning on his way to the stadium he called. My chest felt tight looking at his number light up the screen, and with a smile on my face I answered.

"Did I wake you?"

"No."

He exhaled sharply into the phone. "It's so good to hear your voice, Sweetness. Say you ain't mad at me no more."

"I'd be lying if I said that."

"How you doing?"

"Okay."

"You know how much I love you. Right?"

I coughed. "I thought I did."

"Things are only going to be like this for a little while, but we both have to make the effort to get through this crazy schedule."

"I hear you."

"Shit, not being able to talk to you is driving me crazy. You're on my mind all day. When can I see you?"

"Depends on my workload. Senior year is going to be tougher than I expected. I need to be laser focused if I want to graduate. And plus I have rehearsals, so..."

"So, you're too busy for me? I understand."

I lowered the phone from my ear and scowled wondering, *'What kind of role reversal fuck shit was he playing?'*

"If you have any time to squeeze me in, give me a holler. I sure wanna see you." His voice dragged.

"I feel the same, but if it's only gonna be for a few hours, then..."

"Then it sounds like I have some things to work out to put a smile back on my baby's face. I'll call you after the game. Wish your man luck."

"You've worked your way up the ladder. You got this. Talk to you later."

I watched the tiny uniforms run out of the tunnel on my television with screaming, painted-faced fans going wild in the stands. Longing to see his face in his element, my eyes remained glued to the screen, hoping for a glimpse of Cade standing on the sidelines.

Having talked to him that morning forced me to admit to myself just how bad I missed being in the presence of his charm.

And as I stared at the flashing images of die-hard fans, cheerleaders kicking their legs above their heads, and two gray haired men providing stats about both teams, the cameras suddenly showed a quick shot of him staring at the action on the field.

Seeing his handsome features accented with two wide, black strips drawn below his captivating eyes on the television screen put a big smile on my face, and my back wilted of weakness. I regretted not being there with him.

By the third quarter, I was blessed to see him again along with the rest of the world, fastening his helmet as he ran onto the field.

The commentators began calling out his stats from his college career.

Commentator 1: Number 11 Cade Williamson coming onto the field for Zion Quimby. Quimby led this organization last year as the top Running Back with the highest yards in a rookie season.
Commentator 2: He appears to be leaving the field with a slight limp on his left leg. The team's medics will get a quick look to make sure everything looks good. In the meantime, Cade Williamson, Number 11, is stepping in for Quimby.
Commentator 1: Back in the day they called Williamson, Juke. A second round draft pick that dropped to The Skin's practice team after his first season. Let's see if he's still got the moves.
Commentator 2: Let's see indeed. It's been rumored he's been looking pretty good hence his promotion from the practice squad. No doubt he has chemistry with the team, but I wouldn't want to be in his shoes right now.
Commentator 1: Neither would I. Nothing but pressure on him to show and prove he's still got what it takes to be out there.
Commentator 2: But you know like I know. The ball's gotta get in his hands first.

Hearing them talk about Cade made me nervous. I sat on the

edge of the sofa with shaky legs, happy he'd been given the opportunity to prove himself, but also kicking myself I wasn't there to see him live in action.

The bulky bodies clunked together on the field for a first down picking up ten rushing yards. I locked onto number 11 jogging back into his position. The quarterback shouted military lingo and hand signals. The center chucked the ball behind him to the quarterback, and within the blink of an eye he side passed the ball to Cade. Cade spun around the linebacker in front of him, running sideways towards the sideline until he was pushed out of bounds.

A burst of energy ran through me watching him proudly strut through the players from the opposing team, patting his helmet as he made his way out of their huddle to get back on the field.

Commentator 1: Did you see that!
Commentator 2: We all saw it. Looks like number 11 still has some tricks up his sleeve.
Commentator 1: Let's see if they give him the ball again.
Commentator 2: I believe they will.
Commentator 1: I believe he's showing them they better.

"Hut!" The quarterback yelled. The defense line filled the gaps. On the second "Hut!," the defense stepped into the O line. The quarterback threw the ball from within the pocket behind him to Cade. Cade ran towards the blitz and shimmied past the safety from the opposing team lunging forward towards him. Gaining on him from the side, a Linebacker dove at his feet. Cade swayed to the left, then quickly back to the right, cutting through a hole to keep the ball in play as he took off down the field, running parallel with the sidelines. His teammates ran beside him, knocking the defense down to the green as he carried the ball into the end zone, scoring his first ever touchdown in the league after three years.

The crowd went wild as the team crowded Cade below the

goal, smacking his helmet, and celebrating his play with dance moves.

The network cut to the replay in slow motion.

Commentator 1: Look at the athleticism of Cade 'Juke' Williamson.
Commentator 2: Somebody showed up to the stadium today with a message.
Commentator 1: Oh yeah? What's that?
Commentator 2: Remember me! You thought I was done, but I'm here to prove my being here ain't no fluke! I'm the Juke! Baby!
Commentator 1: He certainly proved himself within minutes of being on the field. I mean look at that agility to slash past the defense to get The Skins six points on the board.

Post-game, he called. "Baby, pack a bag. I'm flying you out here tonight."

"I can't. I have class in the morning."

"I'll pick you up from the airport. We got some making up, planning, and some celebrating to do. Come on. I need you right now."

"I saw you doing your thing today. My TV has been on the sports network showing you in the highlights all evening."

"So, you saw your boy shakin' 'em off?"

"I did. I'm surprised you called. I assumed you'd be out with your friends, or your teammates tonight."

"I'd rather be with you. What'd ya say? Come show me how proud you are of me."

Chapter 16
Cherry Pie

Rays from the sun crept between a slender opening of the drapes. I was still in Cade's arms, waking up to the smell of testosterone blended with smoked wood and powder from his pits. I kissed his naked chest, inhaling all that I missed while he slept with relaxed brows and a look of peace on his face.

With a quick maneuver I climbed on top of him, rolling my hips around his ready woken wood. His lips quivered, then he sighed, opened his eyes, and smiled.

"Mmm." He groaned. "Somebody woke up wanting more of me?" His hands gripped my ass.

I nodded and turned around, sliding my bum towards his face. He reached over to the nightstand and grabbed the leftover chocolate sauce from our midnight dessert. I squeezed my organs and trembled as he poured the thick fudge down the line of my ass.

Gently, he spread my cheeks apart. "Don't scream too loud."

The combination of chocolate lube and a stern tongue stripped my vocals. I shrieked and moaned of pleasure by way of his thirsty tongue, parting my brown sea of flesh. A chill shivered down my spine from the ravenous attention of Cade's mouth searching for the depth of my darkness.

His slippery hands smeared the drippings around my soft bun, clutching it with open palms. I writhed a few body rolls to saturate his face with my sweet, molten infused pearls, then slid down his chest and posed on the flat of my feet.

Dropping down on his eager dick, I squeezed my pussy tight around his pipe. "We've gotta stop meeting like this, Mr. Williamson."

He smacked his lips and lent me an assist, clutching my ass cheeks and bouncing me up and down to the slow grinding rhythm of his liking. "Don't you ever say that shit again." He slapped my ass and his dick traced each side of my walls like it was a gear shift.

"Oh shit," I bellowed. "Your feet's not the only part of you that knows how to move."

His palm roamed back into position. "It's this good pussy I'm in."

"Do that again," I commanded him.

His dick shifted side to side as it delved upward.

"Yes!" I screamed.

The lateral motion of his head banging the sides of my walls took my breath away. In that moment I developed a craving for him. A need only he could satisfy. A growing obsession to have him more than once every few weeks.

"I was right about you all along." I sighed.

'Juke.'

Over breakfast in the lobby cafe, Cade scrolled through his phone, then guilted me.

"Stay 'til the morning."

I looked away. "I can't keep missing class."

"What's one more day? I'm off, and only need to swing by the warehouse to check on a few things. Other than that, I'm all yours. I get back to ballin' in the morning."

"And I need to get back to schoolin' today. Don't I get credit for flying in late last night?"

"You get all the credit." He placed his hand on top of mine in the center of the table. "You've been making a mufucka feel like he's loved since the moment I met you."

"Because I do."

Cade kissed the tips of my fingers. "I'll be glad when you walk across that stage, and you and I don't have to be so far apart."

"Me, too."

The late night sweet nothings and heavy deposits in my checking account continued over the next few weeks. Then, Spencer and Porsha swung through the Nam to drive us up for a big rival game. Friday night we bowled on a double date, and Saturday I third wheeled.

On Sunday, we viewed the game from skybox seats sitting high above raging fans like royalty looking down at everyone.

"I would have felt out of place sitting in here with all these strangers if you and Spencer didn't come with me."

"Look at your cousin over there making friends like he ain't even here with us."

"How much you wanna bet they're over there measuring dicks over who knows the most football stats, and which one of them is friends with the best player on the team."

Together we snickered.

"Pussy by default groupies. Bunch of assholes." Porsha sucked her teeth.

A low chortle escaped my mouth. "That they are, I am sure."

"That's not nice." A deep voice rang from behind us.

Porsha turned around.

"Who asked you?" She grinned on the side of her mouth.

The gentleman laughed. "I was just joshing. Tryna get you ladies attention."

"So you like trouble?" Her brows raised.

"Oh no. Nothing like that. I actually thought what you two said was funny."

"Which part?" I asked, facing the field.

"The bunch of assholes part."

Porsha lowered her brows and turned back around to watch the game. "It was funny because it's true."

Spencer caught a glimpse of our interaction with the funny guy. He moseyed over with his eyes fixated on the man.

"Y'all alright over here?" he asked.

"Peachy." Porsha moaned. "Your friends might miss you if you stay over here too long."

Spencer answered her with his eyes still on the stranger. "Don't start, girl. We ain't local right now."

My eyes enlarged and my chest tightened. "Cous, we are fine over here. No need for none of that."

Spencer tapped my shoulder and rejoined the men huddled near the glass. Porsha and I snickered at his jealousy when he walked away. I turned around to view the threat, and understood why he felt the need to announce himself as an alpha. He sensed the presence of another alpha making himself known.

The stranger's knees were pressed against my seat so I gathered he was tall. His silky, coffee brown skin was strikingly smooth that water would run off of him. Below the brim of a baseball cap, his matching umber colored eyes glowed against the flashing lights from the prompter, and the sparkle of two diamond earrings shone when the light hit them.

"Sorry about my cousin. He's a tad bit territorial of his girl. Thanks for not escalating that."

He smiled. "I knew what I was doing."

"I don't follow."

Gazing into my eyes he said, "I wanted to know if you were here with one of them." His head signaled towards the huddle, then he pointed his finger at Porsha. "I know she is. What's your name?"

I stuttered. "Um..."

"She's spoken for." Porsha tapped my leg and pointed to the field.

"Nice chatting with you." I smiled back at him and turned around.

Porsha whispered, "Girl, don't fuck up these seats."

As the clock wound down to the team's victory, Spencer joined his new comrades in possession of special passes to walk onto the field and enter the tunnel.

The brown babe sitting behind me walked steps ahead of us leaving the skybox. *'I was right. He is tall,'* I said to myself. He took one final look back at me, waved, then disappeared into the crowd.

Porsha rolled her eyes. "You ain't missing nothing there. He's probably an asshole, too. Just like your cousin. We should have gone down to the field with him."

I sighed. "Let Spencer have this one. It looks like a hassle to go down there. And in heels? I have no desire to get caught in that mess."

"Have this one? Chile, your cousin's slick ass is down there trying to get a closer look at those damn cheerleaders."

My bottom lip expanded. "I didn't think about that. Thanks for putting that thought in my head. I wonder if Cade is fucking one of them."

"Damn. My bad. I should have kept that to myself."

Spencer found us an hour later sitting on the corner near the south gate. Porsha was fuming when he slid into the car, but quickly changed her demeanor when he looked at her with raised eyebrows and exhaled sharply from his mouth.

He placed his hand on her leg. "Let's head back to the 'tel."

"How was it down there?" I asked.

Spencer answered me, purposefully avoiding eye contact. "Cameras everywhere."

"You think I'll get to see him before we check out?"

"I'on know cous. Everyone wants a piece of him. His hands are full if you ask me."

"Porsha you were right. We should have gone down there with him."

Spencer looked at Porsha with a funny look on his face.

"Well, did you get to talk to him?" I followed.

"We chatted."

Porsha knocked on my door less than two minutes after we returned from the game. The look Spencer had on his face, was now written across hers.

"I hate this shit, sis."

I sighed. "Are you two fighting?"

"I wish." She closed the door. "Remember when I said not to let Cade see you get angry?"

"Yeah. I've kept my cool. Why?"

"What I'm about to tell you is going to make that difficult, but there's something you need to know...Not unless you already know." Her voice heightened.

I scowled. "Know what?"

"About Cade."

"What is it? Did he get injured or something?"

"Not yet." She took a deep breath. "Cade is married."

Chapter 17
Skin

A heavy skip stunted my heartbeat. From the corner of my eye, I looked at the red numbers change on the clock, then back at Porsha twisting the side of her mouth with her eyes glued on me.

"No, he's not." I scrunched my face.

Porsha stood stone faced with stern eyes. If I had told a joke right then, her lips wouldn't have cracked anything resembling joy. So I smiled, waiting to hear she was pulling my leg.

A full sixty seconds of silence crept between us before she spoke.

"J.C., you know your cousin. You couldn't tell he was acting strange when he got in the car?"

"I picked up on that."

"Spencer said he was telling him how he appreciated the way he treated you, and thanked him for the seats. Cade looked like he had seen a ghost and pulled him to the side, and in a hurry he told him that he loves you, and never meant to hurt you, and he didn't know how to tell you he was married. Then a girl walked up on them, and he introduced her as his wife."

I fell faint. "His wife? Spencer saw this jack in the box wife?"

Porsha nodded.

"What did she look like? Scratch that. I don't wanna know."

"I didn't ask. I came straight over to tell you because Spencer said he couldn't."

I scowled as a scoff left my mouth. "I don't believe this cocka-mamie bullshit. There is no way he's married. If he's not man enough to break up with me, and has to come up with this lame excuse to stop seeing me, then he is a sad sap sucka. And a coward. I mean how weak do you have to be to create a fake wife to end a relationship. We live in different states for God's sake. All he'd have to do is stop calling me and blow me off. I'd get the point."

"J.C., did you not hear the part where he said he loves you? He doesn't want to break up with you. He just couldn't hide the truth any longer."

"Cade can't be married. I sent letters to his house. I've been to his house. I've met the uncle he cares for, who knows me by the way. Why would he show me where he lives when I could poten-tially blow up his spot?"

Porsha shook her head. "Like I said earlier. Bunch of assholes. His uncle is covering for him, and he probably took you to his house."

I hit my forehead with my palm. "Okay Porsha, stop talking for a second."

"I'm not the enemy. I'm helping you piece this shit together."

"But this makes no sense. What kind of married man spends the holidays away from his family? Mary J. Blige said it best. Ain't no happy holidays when you are the side piece. How the fuck am I a side piece? This man has spent Memorial Day, Fourth of July, and Labor Day with me."

"Not all of Labor Day." Porsha reminded me. "The real ones are coming up and y'all have gotten close. He can't get away for the two big ones coming up. He wanted you to be on board before they come rolling in. Sneaky ass bastard."

My face fell from the revelation. Silently, I sulked as my world suddenly crashed like a dummy in a test car with my head spinning of disillusion and lies I'd been told. I felt desolate. Dumb. Defeated.

The world stopped turning, and my vision transitioned from red to funeral black. I seethed with anger flowing through my veins, and saw maroon colored drops of blood falling from a black sky when it was vividly clear and sunny outside. My hand covered my left breast, massaging the pain surrounding my heart. Then, I pictured his face made of gray clouds in the dark sky only my eyes were privy to.

The thought of Cade and a faceless woman felt like a knife piercing my skin. I rubbed my arms, my chest, and my back, pacing the floors of my hotel room, clueless of what to think, and what to do.

"If you wanna fuck him up, we can do that. Spencer might be fond of him, but Butterball and Man will tussle with him if you say the word. And you know Norrie didn't like his ass no way."

Porsha's voice faded as I sat on the sill of the window, imagining he was parking his car in the lot to run inside and tell me this was all some sort of mistake. She called my name several times, but I couldn't speak. I was lost in the daydream of him taking my pain away.

"J.C., breathe."

I gasped. "This man met my family, tells me he loves me all damn day."

"I've seen you two together. I think he does."

"Porsha, please. I know you ain't taking up for him?"

"I would never. I'm just stating what I've seen."

"What you've seen! His tongue was literally up my ass a few weeks ago!"

Porsha snickered. "I'm not laughing at the situation. I'm laughing at you getting turned out."

I peered at her. "Seriously?"

"I'm sorry." Her snickers turned into a roaring laugh. "The way you said it made me picture you two going at it, and…That must have been some experience." She muffled her chuckles.

"If you and Spencer don't mind, I'd like to get out of here."

"Let's do it."

A tear fell from one of my eyes as I stared at the skyline of faded buildings spread across the backdrop of the horizon. Angrily, I packed my bags and felt a change sweep over me once I threw them in the trunk.

I looked back at the city slowly coming back into color as we skirted down the highway. The further away we drove, the easier it became to accept the man I thought who was my person, was nothing more than a façade on two wheels I wished I hadn't met.

The hurt conquered my repressed rage, and I entered into a period of bitterness. Some mistook it for maturity, but I knew better.

For weeks I didn't understand why I didn't lose my shit, and go into a raging fit from the heartbreak. I took the loss and carried on as if nothing had happened, reacquainting myself with life as a single woman. Something I had apparently been for the past few months without realizing it.

"I owe you an apology." Thedé circled the top of her mug with her finger. "I thought you and the football jerk were just a fling. I see now, I was wrong. I should have been more supportive."

"What makes you say this now?"

"You. Your response to him hurting you. You have never reacted this calmly when someone has done wrong by you. You really loved him. I'm sorry."

"Still love him, unfortunately."

"Have you talked to him?"

"No, and I don't plan on it. He leaves so many messages it feels like I talk to him every day."

"Why do you torture yourself? Hit delete and start the healing process."

I shrugged my shoulders. "A part of me still yearns to hear his voice. Especially on the nights I can't sleep."

She leaned forward. "You gotta start over at some point."

I took Thedé's advice and traced the erase messages button on my machine when I got home. But I couldn't do it. I played them as background noise while reading the love letters he sent with cards on top of cards, and gifts from ritzy department stores.

'I never meant to hurt you, Sweetness.
I feel sick without you.
Please forgive me. I love you'.

And my favorite of all:

'I'm my happiest when I'm with you.
I miss you so much.
Please talk to me.
I'm losing my mind not hearing your voice.
Have I ever told you I love you?'

I devoured the love he professed on the page with tears falling from my eyes, and I believed his words to be true. As foolish as it felt to admit that his outcry confused me, and fucked up my ability to think clearly, beneath the hurt and humiliation I found myself doing mathematical equations in search of one answer. Can you love two people at the same time?

The next time he rang, I answered his call. The familiar sound of machinery, and echoed voices joking in the background of the warehouse rattled on as I waited to hear the raspy voice that damaged me.

"I'm sorry," he said, moments after listening to me breathe quietly into the phone. "I never meant to hurt you."

"But you did."

"I know, baby, I know. How have you been?"

I sighed. "I think you can answer that yourself."

"The sound of your voice like this makes me hate myself."

"You should."

"J.C., I made a mistake. I didn't know what to do."

"Well, let me tell you. You wear your ring, you open your mouth, and you say I'm married."

"There was never a right time. Things with us happened so fast, and I was selfish, and got to know you, and couldn't go back to a life without you in it."

"Jesus, Cade. I have so many questions."

"If I love you is one of them. Yes. I love you. You know I do."

"And her?"

"J.C."

"Don't tell me you love us both, because I have been wrestling with that idea for weeks. It doesn't seem possible to me, but do tell me, Cade. Is it? Do you love your wife and me?"

The phone fell silent.

"So, you won't answer then?"

His silence stung my ears. It felt like a poisonous dart had found its way to my weakened soul with just the right amount of venom to put me out of my misery. I believed he did love me, but couldn't fathom how it was possible to hurt me all the same, and suddenly the answers to my questions didn't matter.

"Cade."

"Yes, Sweetness."

My voice wavered. "I wish you nothing but the best in life."

"I'm my best when I'm with you. I know you love me just as much as I love you. Stop pretending you hate me all of a sudden."

"I don't hate you. I want to. But for some reason I don't yet understand, I can't find it in me to loathe your very existence after what you've done to me."

Cade tapped the phone against the wall. "Tell me you still love me."

"I love you." I took a long pause. "Take care of yourself. Good-bye," I whimpered as I ended the call.

He dialed me back twice more overnight. I cried listening to the sixty second silent message of him breathing, making up the words he could have said. The words I wanted to hear, knowing they would be futile.

Then his second message gutted me to my core.

"You'll never stop being my Sweetness.
And I'll never stop loving you."

From that moment on, I chose to remember the guy with the captivating eyes I met one hot summer night on the crowded streets of the beach as Cade. But the guy who broke my heart, and duped me into believing I knew what love was, would forever be remembered as the man who ran the trick play on me. A man I would always remember as Juke.

Chapter 18
Be That Easy

The big three were disastrous. Thanksgiving was a reminder of how important family is, with a line of questioning from my Uncle Cole about the football tickets he was promised. Spencer was no help adding fuel to the fire, bragging about the sky box, and going on the field.

As the two of them argued, I eased out of the house like a thief in the night.

Shawnnie followed me outside. "Where is pretty boy?"

"He is with his family, and I am with mine."

She scoffed. "You think I don't know something is up?" She held up one of Ma's bread pudding dishes with shit stirring eyes.

"How did you manage to get this past her?" I pinched off a piece with my fingers.

"The same way I come in late and never wake her. I'm good at what I do."

"Couldn't swindle a fork?"

She sucked her teeth. "I was working fast. So, what's the story? You ain't change your phone number for nothin'. Did pretty get tired of driving this far for some pussy?"

"Un uh." I moaned below a sigh.

"Then what is it, 'cause I know he fucked up?"

"That he did. He's married."

Shawnnie swung her fists in the air. "I knew it was something sheisty about that dude. Motherfucker came down here in a fisherman's hat, chaps shirt, and big ass drug dealer chain. He probably shipped his wife and their fifty-leven kids to Six Flags to come down here for some fresh young ass."

I glared at her reaction.

"Sorry, sis." She patted my leg.

"Are you? I can't really tell."

"I'm not gonna rag on you when you're suffering from a broken heart. Not unless you knew he was married. Then I would..."

I cut her off. "I didn't know. How could I? He stayed on the phone with me day and night, treated me well, spent every available moment he had with me. Where was this woman?"

"Tucked away somewhere believing his lies like you were. Men are shit. Married or not, he was gonna be fucking someone else living that far away."

"Yeah. I know the line from *Something About You*. '"If a man ain't lying next to you, he's lying next to someone else."'"

"Bingo." Shawnnie shot her fingers to the sky. "And in your case, he was lying next to his wife." She shook her head.

"He used to tell me he loved me all the time. And I felt like he did. But how is it possible to have a whole wife at home, but you claim you love me? It doesn't make sense."

Shawnnie kissed her teeth. "Contrary to what some people believe, you can love two people at the same time. You just love one more than the other."

"And since when have I ever enjoyed being second?" I sucked my fingers clean.

"Never." She rubbed my back. "You alright though?"

"I will be." My voice dragged. "I miss him. I loved everything about him, even if it was a lie."

"I don't know if it was love, sis, but he felt something for you. I saw the way he looked at you. Crippling you with those cat eyes." Shawnnie chuckled. "He gave you that look that weakens every woman's knees."

"And he did," I said, smacking on more pudding. "You ever had your ass ate?"

Shawnnie choked and chortled. "Un uh. Spare me the details."

Our laughter echoed so loudly, Ma heard us on the porch. She opened the door and we hid the pudding behind us on the wicker chair.

"Get back in the house and stop being anti-social," Ma fussed.

"Yes ma'am," we said, wiping tears from our eyes.

Ma turned up her lip and creased her forehead. "Both of you have bread pudding on your lips," she said, then closed the door.

Shawnnie nudged my arm. "My job here is done. I got you to laugh. Now promise me you won't give that married asshole your power."

"What do you mean?"

"You've allowed him to put your light out. You let him change you. You've always been bubbly and outgoing and spirited. The last time you came home you were mean. Even on this break, you've been quiet, and haven't smiled as much. Take your power back. He ain't worth you losing yourself."

Going home for Christmas break nearly broke me. Lectures from every woman in my family peeled my already thin skin into a glass onion. They yapped on and on about my coming home alone.

"Is the boy coming?" Aunt Wil asked.

Cousin Babs cut in. "Men spend the holidays with their number one. Them other ones get the day after."

"I am single. No one is coming."

"Good riddance!" Norrie yelled. "I didn't like his ass."

"Norrie, that was no secret." I sighed. "And I'm not going to sit around and talk about the breakup either. Can we talk about something else?"

My confession didn't stop the whispers that carried on from Christmas to New Years. And with Juke's team in the playoffs, I stayed away from the bars to keep him out of sight and out of mind.

Thedé insisted I get out of the house and come out with her to a client's shindig. I did, and overheard a conversation between two men discussing The Skins had lost the Eastern Conference Championship.

The petty in me celebrated for a moment. But the empath in me pulled out my phone, and watched the news footage of the team being interviewed about their loss.

He nearly took my breath away when the recording switched to him seated in front of the team's logo plastered in the backdrop. Below a Skins stocking cap, his hurting eyes avoided the cameras behind a microphone. His voice sent chills down my spine. I could feel his disappointment as he took the blame for letting his team down on a play where his foot went out of bounds.

'*Karma is a bitch,*' I thought to myself, while pretending the flutters in my chest weren't a tell that I felt sorry for him.

It saddened me that he'd lost. Almost enough for my pride to step aside and let me foolishly call him.

The strength I showed by refraining made me proud. I carried on with my healing, and by spring, the flowers were back to blooming, and the April showers cleansed the dirt off my path, and gave me a new road to ease down.

Chapter 19
Kiss of Life

At the start of summer, the talk of Bikers Weekend began circling around.

"I'mma sit this one out." I told Kool.

Then Thedé suggested we go. "You know you want to. Last year was last year, and this time I'll be there to make sure everything goes smoothly. Let's go and make new memories."

"Why the sudden interest?"

"Eight Letters."

I scowled. "I love you?"

Thedé cracked with snickers. "No, girl. Free Room. LaTreece, my co-worker, invited us to stay in her family's timeshare."

"That's a hard deal to pass up."

"Is that a yes?"

I smiled on the side of my mouth. "When do we leave?"

―――――

I didn't expect anxiety to overwhelm me when we arrived. The girls toured the streets without me while I settled in the room, looking at the flashy cars strolling by, girls dancing in the street, and enjoying the breeze from the ocean up high on the balcony until the sun fell behind the ocean.

Hours later they returned wound up and ready to party.

Thedé wrestled me to the ground. "We didn't come here for you to be held up in this room all weekend. Put on something sexy. I have a surprise for you."

"Whatever scheme you've concocted, cancel it. I'm good."

"Get out of these house clothes and put on something cute."

LaTreece threw my bag on the bed. "She's right. It's lively out there. You need to be amongst it and have fun. It's why we're here."

I pushed Thedé off of me and pointed to her. "I take it she didn't tell you what happened the last time I came here to have fun?"

LaTreece shook her head side to side.

I huffed. "Tell me what the surprise is and I'll think about it."

Thedé grabbed my shoulders. "Scott and Townes are in a hotel a few blocks from here with a few friends."

"I didn't come here to make the same mistake, Thedé."

"We're just going to say hi, introduce LaTreece, and stay for a few minutes. Now let's go. You've been in here all day."

"Okay. I'll get dressed."

"Good. Meet us in the lobby. Members get to enjoy a free cocktail mixer in the lounge."

I threw on a pair of black jeans and a thin crop top, pulled the holder from my ponytail, and let my hair down to blow in the wind.

LaTreece laughed when I arrived in the lounge. "What the hell do you have on?"

"What's wrong with this?"

"We're at the beach. I'm walking around with my ass hanging out and you put on jeans."

"I've done this before. It gets chilly at night. Either I go like this, or I go back upstairs."

Thedé threw her hands up. "At least you're out of the room."

The air smelled the same as it did every year. Marijuana, canned air freshener, and the smell of electricity lined every corner. Cheap perfume blended with burning exhaust fumes from motorcades clouding the streets, and streams of salt water ribboned in between with clean air.

When the horns from cars and bikes blew, every girl turned to see if it was them being catcalled. It was the same every year, and though I wasn't thrilled to be a part of the chaos and bad decisions waiting to happen, I was amused watching Thedé and LaTreece enjoy themselves from the attention of thirsty men looking for a good time.

Bypassing countless parking lots during our trek, the freedom of women partying in the street, and dancing to the bass lines booming from parked cars put the first smile on my face of the night.

LaTreece yelled over the crowds and music, "The further we walk inland, the better the fun. It's boring on our side,"

"Trust me. That is a good thing. You'll see," I said, stopping abruptly between two hotels as my eyes locked with a familiar set. "Cade." I mouthed below my breath.

His eyes widened, brows raised, and lips parted. "J.C."

I read his lips call my name and I shivered. We turned around at the same time, then he tapped the arm of his friend, matching every step I took towards him.

Less than an inch apart, we stood in front of a crowd that went silent in my ears with nothing but the beating of our hearts making music inside my head.

He was once again within my reach. Chills covered my body. My nipples pebbled through my chiffon top, and I wanted to jump his bones right then and right there in front of everyone.

The look in his eyes said the same. We gazed into each other's eyes, engrossed with the bond that never truly broke between us. Saying everything we left unsaid without words.

Our connection was still there. The need waiting to be explored. The desire at its peak. The bond still strong.

He grinned on the side of his mouth as a breeze wafted his manly, woodsy scent into my nose. Immediately, I was charged with memories of how he cared for me when we were together. How I would have stood ten toes for him. How complete I felt in his arms.

What were the odds we would run into each other when millions of people horded the streets? If love wasn't the reason, chance was playing games with my heart because cupid had shot his arrow in me once again.

Standing still in the quiet, he knew I hadn't gotten over him. We bent our heads forward and kissed with a hundred eyes watching the magnetic attraction we abandoned make up for lost time. He wrapped his arms around me and pulled me close. Still hungry for me.

My hunger was all the same. I placed my hands against his chest and held back tears, locking onto the full, sweet, lying lips I missed and craved on my skin.

A tap hit my shoulder and the sound of our audience returned. A woman's voice in the background said, "What the fuck is happening right now? Did I stumble into *The Bold and the Beautiful,* or is it normal for people to see each other on the street and just start making out?"

Cade and I laughed into each other's mouths.

He leaned back and weakened my spine with two words. "Hey, Sweetness."

Thedé cleared her throat. "J.C., what the hell are you doing? Everyone's staring."

"Thedé, meet Juke."

Her mouth dropped open. "You're the infamous asshole..." She scoffed, rolled her eyes, then glared at me. "Maybe I shouldn't have forced you to come out tonight. I'll be over there with LaTreece waiting on you."

"Juke? Since when do you call me that?" Cade furrowed his brows.

I bit my lip and twisted in his arms.

"I miss you." He bit my cheek.

I squealed and squirmed. "I miss you, too."

"I didn't think I would ever see you again."

"Me either. You can thank my friend." I pointed behind me.

"The one who just called me an asshole, or the other one?"

I chuckled. "The one who called you an asshole. I had no intention of ever setting foot out here again. But she begged me to come this weekend."

He looked past me in her direction and nodded. "Thank her for me. I would, but it's clear what she thinks of me."

Thedé gave him a long eye roll as she tapped her wrist.

"Where are you headed?" he asked.

"To meet some of her friends. How about you?"

"Looking for one of mine with the keys to my truck. When I find him, can I pick you up, and go for a drive?"

"I'd like that."

He planted another open mouthed kiss on my lips.

"You look different. Still gorgeous, but different."

"You didn't hang around long enough to see my hair straightened."

"I like it." He ran his fingers through the end of my tresses.

I ran my fingers down the center of his shirt. "You've picked up some weight. Life's been good to you then?"

"It is right now."

"Juke, man, come one!" his friend yelled.

"Baby, I need to get this fool off my back. I would call you, but you changed your number on me."

I lowered my forehead to his chin. "If yours is still the same, I'll call you."

"You remember it? I mean, I can't tell. I haven't heard from you." He pinched my ass.

"We'll talk."

"Don't take too long. I'll be waiting."

Thedé gave me a disappointing stare as I approached her and LaTreece. With a huge smile plastered on my face, and chills crawling down my back in the dead of heat, I felt alive. It was as if the colors in a rainbow had faded to shades of gray since the breakup, and suddenly burst with vibrancy, playing a blended melody from each arch.

"Since when did you start making out with people in the middle of the street?" Thedé questioned me.

I walked past them in a daze as if we weren't wandering the street together.

"Well?" She badgered me, creeping on my heels.

I paused my steps. "How much further do we have to walk?"

LaTreece beamed at me. "Someone seems like a totally different person. Who was that?"

Thedé cut me off. "That was an asshole." She grabbed my hand and raised it above my head. "And this is a damn fool in love with it."

Chapter 20
Soldier of Love

I was in a fool's paradise walking between a smiling face on my left, and a tight, scowling face on my right. I sensed a lecture coming from LaTreece, stomping on my side like she lost money.

"He got you open. I've never seen you make out in public like that. Please tell me you're not thinking what I think you're thinking." Thedé sighed.

I giggled and curved the side of my mouth. "What am I thinking?"

"Oh fuck. Never mind. That little snickering right there lets me know you're about to go down the wrong road."

LaTreece smiled in my face. "I can't blame her. He was putting out all the right vibes. And definitely a looker. I wanna know the story, 'cause that was some crazy, romantic shit that fell out of the sky. My heart was pounding watching you two go at it."

"Trust me, LaTreece. Don't put any fuel on that fire." Thedé wrapped her arm around my shoulder, and her hips rubbed against mine. "What'd he say?"

"Just that he misses me."

"And?" LaTreece's skinny arm wrapped around mine.

"That he wants to see me later."

Thedé placed her hand on her chest. "I beg you. Don't go."

"Relax. The ball is in my court. He doesn't have my number. I have to call him. And whatever I decide, don't judge me. Just be my friend."

Thedé didn't need to know my mind was already made up. I was going to make that call, and I was going back down the wrong road.

The presence of Cade didn't work well for Townes either. I nitpicked everything about him, watching his every move, searching for inconsistencies and unattractive qualities. He was near perfect on the surface, minus the constant checking of his phone when he thought no one was paying attention to him.

When I looked at him all I saw was my Aunt Wil preaching, "If he's smooth on the surface, the shit is underneath." And she was right. I caught him checking out Thedé's voluptuous ass when she followed Scott into the kitchen for more beer, and the red flag had been raised.

Coming close to an hour of watching LaTreece mingle with a drink in her hand the entire time, laughter from the kitchen came to a halt. Whether it was demon time against the fridge, or not, I excused myself outside to take in the oceanside view from the top floor.

Townes popped outside shortly after. "I have to know. Why haven't we hit it off?"

I shrugged my shoulders.

"I thought I made it obvious that I like you. And I thought I felt a little vibe from you when we met, so what am I doing wrong?"

"Nothing."

"Then go out with me."

"Umm. I don't know."

Townes sighed. "So, I am doing something wrong."

"It's not you."

He interrupted. "Don't say it's you."

"But it is, mostly."

"Thedé told me a little something something about you." He checked his phone.

"Did she?" I raised my brows.

He lowered his head and looked up at me. "She said you were hung up on a married man. That can't be true. Is it?"

"You mean like you're hung up on how many times her ass bounces whenever she walks by."

Townes coughed. "Say what now? Whoa. Whoa. I'm not into Thedé, she's got Scott by the balls. But let's be honest for a second. How can anyone miss that ass?" he said, through the goofiest grin.

A light chuckle escaped my lips. "Yes, she has a head turner. But my question to you is why don't you know when and when not to look?"

The goofy grin fell on his face and he tapped the screen of his phone until it lit up.

"But say no more. I see now that you share the same quality of other men. You're the type that can't help yourself. And I'm hoping to meet someone who can."

"No, no. I didn't mean it like that. What I was trying to say was, I know you look at it too because it's hard to miss."

He and I laughed.

"Throw a penny and you'll see pretty women and big asses. They're everywhere. So why can't a man let one pass by without gawking at it like a blind man suddenly gaining sight. Especially when he's shooting his shot with someone he says he "likes." I quoted with my fingers. "Is in the room?"

"That sounds like a trick question, and I've already said too much. I'mma quit while I'm ahead and press reset."

"No need for a reset. I thought when you asked what you were doing wrong, I could be honest with you."

"Is that the only thing?"

I pressed my lips together.

"So, what's the truth about this man stupid enough not to choose you?"

I huffed. "There was someone in the picture that didn't turn out to be who they said they were. Thedé should have told you the whole story if she was gonna be out here airing out my business."

"Shit. Once again I've said too much. Don't think she was airing out your business. I asked her if someone was in my way, and she said, "Not anymore. The man blocking your chance is off the market and off her radar. Give her time. She'll come around." I figured it's been a minute since we last saw each other, and as you said, I'm shooting my shot."

I stood on my tiptoes and kissed his cheek. "You check the boxes, Townes. But the timing is all wrong."

"Well if it's timing, I'm a patient man."

I smiled. "I'll keep that in mind. One more thing. Stop looking at your phone every five minutes."

His eyes shifted from side to side.

"I know you're a businessman, but at this hour, you're checking for a sure thing even though you invited me over."

He rubbed the crown of his head with both hands, then slipped the phone in his back pocket. "Damn, you really are on my ass tonight."

"That's not my intention, because I do like you, but at least when I was with the married man, I had all of his attention. I can't seem to keep yours."

Townes followed me back inside, pressing on my heels and tugging at my fingers. LaTreece was curled up on the sofa getting cozy with one of his friends. I pointed to the kitchen and she gave me a thumbs up.

I chuckled through a grin. "I'll see y'all back at the room when you're done over here."

She nodded.

Townes sighed. "J.C., you don't have to run off."

I placed my hand on the knob.

"At least let me walk you back to your place."

"Thanks, but no thanks. I'll be fine. You have some calls to make." I clicked my teeth.

'And so do I.'

Chapter 21
In Another Time

Amongst a collective of bad decisions in the making, I was face to face with my forbidden lover's gaze. His fingers entangled with mine as his chest stuck out from taking a deep breath.

"Did I get here fast enough?" he asked.

I shook my head. "No."

He smiled. "As I waited for you to call me, I got to thinking. This right here. You and me. We're meant to be. Us running into each other in a huge crowd like that tells me all I need to know."

"I was thinking the same thing."

He looked behind him. "Let's take a walk before we get out of here."

I followed him to the beach, wrapped in his arms as the cold breeze dusted strands of sand across our feet, and the mist of the waters frizzed my hair. The invigorating scent of his natural odor mixed with the warm notes of his cologne danced around me, playing a memory game in my mind as we walked closer to the waves rolling ashore.

As the beige sand turned to brown mud, flashes of our caper

brought a smile to my face while he shared what life had been like for him over the past few months.

"I'm on the trade list. Charlotte is looking pretty good for my future. And I hope the deal works out because then I'll be closer to you."

"I graduated. I'm moving out of North Carolina in a few weeks."

"Come to Charlotte. I can take care of you."

"I know you can, but I'm good taking care of myself."

"So I see. You lookin' good, baby. Especially in this moonlight." He unbuttoned his shirt and draped it around me. "You have no idea how many nights I've dreamed about you." He pulled me closer. "I still love you, J.C."

My eyes invited him to kiss me. His lips parted mine and drew my tongue into his mouth. The heat from his strong arms and the blood racing inside my veins warmed me inside and out. His shirt folded over his arm as he pressed my lower back, driving me further into his swollen chest. The firmness of his cock pricked my lower abdomen, and I sighed in his mouth feeling as though I couldn't get enough of his kisses.

His hands reached lower, palmed my ass, and lifted my body. I wrapped my legs around him, thrusting on his hardness with my pussy clutching on it through our clothes.

"If I had on a bathing suit, I'd let you pull it to the side and bounce me up and down your dick right here, right now."

"And for you, I'd risk the jail time. Let's get out of here."

We raced out of the sand. He waited for me at the gated entrance and took my hand, leading me to his bike parked in the lot. I wrapped my arms around his chest and held onto him with a snug grip. The vibe of déjà vu made me feel like all was right with the world as we sped down open streets with the wind blowing through my already ruined hair.

The roads had cleared as the night was near morning. He

pulled into a reserved resort lot next to a fancy truck and trailers lined up in rows.

"This is me." He pointed to the overly accessorized truck.

"There was nothing wrong with the other one."

He unlocked the doors and helped me inside. "I would have given it to you, but you wouldn't take anything from me. I miss that feeling."

"What feeling is that?"

"Knowing somebody loves me for me, and not for what I have, or what I can do."

I scooted over.

He hopped in. "Now if I recall, you said something about bouncing up and down on my..."

I hurdled on top of him. We clashed into each other's arms, expelling passions beyond borders.

Between kisses he whispered, "I've missed you so much. You have no idea how crazy I've been without you."

I panted into his mouth while struggling to pull down my pants. "I missed you, too. Now shut up and show me you still love me."

I raised my head towards the moonroof. He tugged at my waist, then used his strength to rip off my pants. Cade bent my back and my face rested on the dash. He threw my panties next to my face and tasted what he missed. I called out his name, steady in his hands like a stage built for his performance.

The softness of his tongue exploring the lines and curves of my pussy brought a tear to my eye. I watched my faded reflection in the windshield melded with the stars in the dark blue sky smiling down on me— high on love, emotion, passion, and lust. He sucked on my drip with such tenderness, I began to feel as though I was floating high above, able to touch the very stars witnessing my indiscretion without judgment.

Cade pulled me forward and sat me on his dick. "Ah." He

exhaled, securing he wouldn't slip out of me with a heavy hand on my ass.

I moaned from the penetration, clenching my walls around his stiffness. A tingling sensation sent chills all over my back as he punctured the pussy he abandoned like a spry third leg that could walk on water, taking steps in my pond, fearless and proud.

My hands clung to his shoulders as he rolled my ass around his cock to the tempo of my hips in motion.

"This tight pussy was waiting for Daddy to come home. She ain't stopped jumping yet." He grinned, then gently bit my shoulder. "Daddy's home, Sweetness."

My head pressed against the foggy glass above me. Cade pressed the button to turn on the car, then opened the roof so we could breathe.

I held him close as I fucked him, savoring every millisecond of the moment to my memory. He tugged the nape of my hair and lowered the back of my head to the seat, and bent my legs past my chest.

Sitting on his knees, he hovered above me, paused, then gazed into my eyes. A hard stroke pushed the top of my head into the passenger door. A second stroke reached the height of my yoni.

"Umph." He sighed, pounding into me like a wrecking ball. "Oh, Sweetness. You take this dick like a good girl. Tell me you love it."

"I love it," I whispered.

He licked my lips, groaning like a wounded horse. Fucking me like he owned me. And at that moment, he did. Remembering the pressure points of my pussy, he knew where to strike in my corners to make me shudder on his pipe.

I pushed him back and turned around, tooting my ass in his face. He munched on my wetness, singing into my depth as I balled up against the door.

He slid back inside. "I wanted you to look at me. It's been too long since I've seen your pretty face. But if this is how you want it, I'll give it to you."

I consumed all of him, taking his vigorous jabs while my head banged against the door, and him shaking the truck like a quake was below the ground.

He leaned forward and brushed my hair out of my face. "Look at me."

My eyes shifted into his.

"I still love you," he whined.

I raised my back and smeared the moisture of my face against the window. "I believe you."

"Turn around," he ordered, sliding out of me. "I wanna look at you."

He maneuvered my back against the seat, cuffing my legs at his sides. I pressed on his chest, weakened by the heat between us, still yearning to continue our escapade.

"It's you and me, baby," his voice uttered with sincerity.

"You hurt me, Cade," I muttered, rocking my hips back and forth, holding my breasts to contain the stinging in my chest.

"I'm sorry I hurt you," he said mid-stroke, circling his pipe around in my world.

A powerful surge of angst and passion mixed with the receiving of good dick overpowered me. My back went numb, my shoulders laxed, and my chest pounded from the fast pace of my beating heart and unresolved feelings.

I covered my face.

"Don't hide from me." His hand brushed below my chin, lifting my face.

Our eyes met and his gaze held mine. Love was present, but so was hurt, misery, pain, and distrust. His hands pressed my ass forcefully against his upper thighs, and he juddered.

"Don't come in me," I warned.

"Don't make me lie to you, J.C. You know your pussy is too

good to pull out." He grazed my nipples with his teeth, refusing to release my ass from his grip.

His strokes intensified, driving deep and rhythmically to the tune of my heartbeat racing against time, and his sighs turned into deep, heavy winded pants. He was close, and I did nothing to stop him. I couldn't. The pleasure was too electrifying. The moment too consuming to end it. The tie between us, sealed.

Lost in the euphoric hunger that distance, lies, and time created, I contemplated welcoming his cream inside of me. His kisses to my neck almost solidified the deal. I was ready to take the chance of creating a life bond with him. Reclaim what had been stolen from me. Wrapped up in his world. Swept up in the idea of us.

His hands slid from my bum and wrapped around my neck. He groaned deep in my ear. "Don't be mad at me, J.C.. I have no control when it comes to you." His cock pumped inside of me faster.

The look in his eyes told me he was going for it. I stared into them until he closed them and frightened myself. I saw life with and without him, the good and the bad, the before and the after, but couldn't decipher the truth from the lies.

I lifted his hand from my neck. He trailed them down towards my breasts and fondled my nipples until they bud, then my breath hitched.

I saw it. The lighter shade of skin on his fourth finger. A detail that hadn't stuck out at me before.

I wanted to kick myself for not thinking to look at it earlier, and I lied to myself that it would have deterred me from being in the compromising position I was in. It wouldn't have. I wanted Cade Williamson the first time I saw him. That fact hadn't changed this time either. I didn't care about the past, or his present when fate brought us together a second time. The look in his eyes when he saw me was all I needed to end up on my back in his truck, straddled to him for minutes of pleasure, and a fresh trip down Memory Lane.

While I enjoyed the poking and prodding of the man they called Juke, a rupture of suppressed emotions rushed to my chest and my throat like a riptide. I realized I didn't know this person giving me unbeknownst pleasure. I only knew a version of him. A fraction of the man he pretended to be. And yet, I still found myself in love with him. But miraculously no longer stupid for him.

Our sweet reunion was a rollercoaster ride. At first I heard the melodic tune of Sade's *Mermaids* playing as the soundtrack of our story in my head. Quickly that tune shifted to D'Angelo's *Shit, Damn, Motherfucker.*

I lifted my hips and arched my back when I felt the head of his dick swell between my slit. My pussy spat him out, and I lowered my body on the seat of his new wheels.

Cade wailed of pleasure and confusion, holding his dick with his free hand, shaking his seeds on my stomach. "Ahhhh." He grunted. "Baby, what's wrong?" His narrowed eyes studied me, having failed to hold my gaze.

"This." I searched his truck for a napkin, a towel, a shirt, anything to clean myself.

Covered in smut, and mentally frazzled by the trace of his water scented chest veiling above the smell of salt water and chlorine smeared on my skin, I made eye contact with him.

His fingers interlaced with mine. "Why did you stop?"

"I never saw it before." I ran my finger across the untanned line on his hand.

He pulled his hand away. "J.C., we just made our way back to each other. Now is not the time to..."

I cut him short. "I think you owe me this conversation."

He sighed and closed his eyes, resting his back in the spot behind the wheel. I cleared his mess with my panties, threw them on him, and pulled up my pants. A red hue formed at his temple. I studied the anger building in him, the swelling of his chest, the stunted breaths, and his pouty lips. All I assumed I chose to ignore before.

"What do you do?" I asked him, reliving the heartbreak that dimmed my light.

"I don't know what you mean?"

"Do you take it off when she's not around? Do you and your wife —God, that hurt me to say out loud — have some sort of under-standing when you travel? Did she know about me? I've imagined so many scenarios in my head."

"I'm not having this conversation."

My eyes burned like lasers at his refusal to answer my ques-tions. It told me he knew what his vows meant, yet he was out with me. It told me I still came second, and as a husband should be with his wife, he was protecting her.

"How can you love me when you're married?"

"Sweetness." He sighed.

"Why did you play with me like that? You could have fucked me that weekend and forgot about me. That, I would have under-stood, but to drag me along for months, and trick me into believing you love me was downright cruel."

"I do love you. I never lied about that."

"Do you know how love works?"

He grabbed my legs and slid me next to him. "Do you?"

"I thought I did."

"J.C., I didn't come here expecting to find a woman that made me feel at ease— that I could laugh with— whose smile made me feel like I was worth a damn. It just happened. Could I have fucked and forgotten you? Yes." He cupped my face and stole my lips with the tenderest kiss. "But after a few hours with you, I couldn't imagine not being in your life. And I still don't."

The buried rage, unreleased anger, high emotions, love and lust blending between our mouths lit a fire in me I couldn't control. The trance his eyes cast upon me still had its effect. The taste of his lips, more addictive.

He squeezed my body and I wilted in his arms, distracted by his bare cock standing at attention for a do-over.

I kicked off my pants as his fingers fucked me hard until I squealed and begged for them to stay pressed against my g-spot. Cade sucked on my neck, applying the proper amount of pressure to make me weak in his grasp.

"Anything for you, Sweetness. I'll do anything for you."

"I like when you make me feel good."

"I *love* when I make you feel good."

As I slid down his dick, I accepted our love was once beautiful, but dimensional. Our dynamic changed me as a person, forced me to grow, and damaged me in the process.

In the recourse of our union, I learned love shouldn't be fucked up like ours. I didn't deserve to be in love with a stranger I could never call my own, torn between glory and madness, even though it felt like paradise. But I dove down that unforbidden road one more time.

The moans and sighs he brought out of me would never be forgotten. The way he caressed my body eased away the suffering he caused me. The waves we rocked in his truck were more than the ones rolling in from the ocean yards away. The steam we created was more than the fog veiling above it.

Cade knew my heart, reaching for it with his wielded sword, piercing my punani with intense wounds to carve his outline in my flesh. I was on top, but he was in control, moving me however he desired, wanted, and intended so that I would be in place to receive his warm load.

With his face connected to my bosom, he shot inside of me and I couldn't move. I was sealed to him. Bonded like glue. Tighter than a rope at a hanging. His body lurched, holding me bound to him by my ass cheeks. I constricted my muscles around his pulsing pipe.

His hands traveled up my back to my shoulders, pressing my body firmer on him.

"You empty that clip yet?"

His warm breath heated my chest as he laughed through a grin. "I could live in you, girl." He dragged his fingers to my neck and choked me lightly. "I can't believe you robbed me of that the first time," he muttered, loosened his grip, then kissed my neck on both sides.

I slipped off of him. "Thank you." I said, stepping into my pants.

"What for?"

"Closure." I zipped up and opened the door.

He slid on his naked ass across the seat and reached for me. "Closure? This morning proves this book ain't closed."

"It is for me."

"No, it's not. You still love me."

My chest pounded as I confessed. "I do. That's why I'm ending this before it starts again."

Cade's eyes gleamed in front of a pink and orange sky and rising sun behind him in the window. Time stood still as I stared into them, feeling my love for him plead his case.

The aches in my chest sank into my quivering stomach while my eyes swallowed my tears. I leaned forward and kissed him. One final lip lock serenaded my lips, and sealed my heart from the hurt that would come from loving him further.

"Maybe it can be you and me in the next life," I said, closing the door of his truck, and on us.

He lowered the window. "You walking away won't stop me from loving you in this one."

My chest caved on the inside as I walked away with his words tattooed on my heart, but I kept my eyes forward, trembling from the pain of his eyes piercing my soul on my every step.

It took strength to ignore my heart, telling me to run back to him, wanting to feel his hands pull on mine, and hear him say something crafty to convince me to change my mind.

I pressed on, listening for the engine to turn, waiting for him to drive away from our toxic love and unbreak the curse he placed on my heart. But he took the easy way out, watching me carry the burden of ending our tale as I walked away from him...from us... and our love forever.

Epilogue
King of Sorrow

I t's funny how a grown woman can tell a young girl what she needs to know to maneuver in a man's world. Advice to bring a man to his knees, and tricks to keep a girl steps ahead of the games men play, only for the young one to ignore words of wisdom, and follow the path of her predecessors— gallivanting through life wanting to be loved, and make decisions based on emotion. I was no different.

Finding myself on the opposite end of such conversations with my daughter and niece on their way to college was a reminder of how clueless I was when I was their age. And how I wished time travel was real so I could go back and erase my regrets that were hard to live with.

My loving husband, Marshall, and Larry, Shawnnie's husband, trailed us across two states to roll tide with the class of 2020. A new generation of relentless dumb asses, hormones on two legs with zero moral compass, and breathing examples of their catch phrase of not giving a fuck.

In my mission of Captain Mom Tries to Save Her Girls From the Hoe Life, adjustments were needed in passing down the jewels of dating my mother and aunts had given to me. My "don't be dumb like me" lectures weren't a match for the chaos of modern society, and, like Shawnnie and myself, our girls ignored every gem and warning.

Shawnnie tapped my hand on the wheel. "J.C., those babies are not listening to shit we're saying. This generation is truly the fuck 'round and find out bunch."

I huffed. "Can't tell them shit."

"When you think about it, they ain't no different from us. Especially you." Shawnnie chuckled. "You did whatever the hell you wanted to."

"Is that right?" Danielle, my daughter, propped in between us.

"So you were listening?" I pinched her cheeks.

"Don't worry about us, Ma. We are not going to school to get pregnant, if we do have sex, we'll use condoms. If we drink at a party, we'll watch our cups with a hawk eye, and we'll never leave each other at a party or walk alone at night."

I mumbled under my breath, "Or do half the stupid shit your mother did."

"What was that?" Shawnnie laughed.

"Nothing."

"No backsies. What did you say, Ma?"

"She said don't be stupid and let a boy tell you he only wants to put the head in."

"Eww, Aunt Shawnnie."

"Ma!" Shawnnie's daughter, Alexandria, hollered.

I added, "I did forget to tell you that one. All the boys try that line, and trust me, it's never just the tip."

"I said don't worry about us." Danielle gritted through her teeth.

"We just want you girls to date nice boys." I looked at Dani in the rearview. "You know, a nice boy who will turn out to be a nice man like your father."

Shawnnie chortled. "Don't listen to her. Your mother dated

asshole after asshole, and almost missed the boat your father was on."

Dani's big eyes grew bigger. "Is that true?"

"Yup." Shawnnie glanced at me. "Your daddy hit on her while she was dating the biggest asshole of them all. And she let him get away. But with your mother's luck, and me and your big cousin Porsha being the crafty women we are, we set them up."

"How?" Dani asked.

I cleared my throat. "Crafty is a stretch. Your Aunt Shawnnie and Cousin Porsha betrayed me. They continued to have a relationship with my ex after we broke up."

Shawnnie cut me off. "That was all Spencer. Spencer betrayed you. Uncle Cole and I just tagged along for the free tickets. But as it turned out, I was meant to be at that game because Marshall was there and asked about you. The rest is history."

I smiled.

Danielle tapped my shoulder. "So who was the ex?"

Shawnnie and I looked at each other and snickered.

"Here's an old school phrase for you. A non-motherfucking factor."

<hr>

The moment I dreaded arrived. My baby, off on her own, living in a co-ed dorm with cute boys, free from my helicoptering.

Shawnnie and I slipped looks at each other like cougars on an open field. The youngins didn't look like the boys when we came up. They had muscles on top of muscles, eight row washboard abs, full beards, and were polite. Too polite.

"Breathe, J.C.. The time has come for you to face it. Our girls are going to have fun in this place. You and I certainly would have." Shawnnie squeezed me with a bear hug until I laughed. "Did you see the one with the earring in his ear? If I could *Freaky Friday* with Alexandria for a weekend I would..."

I kicked my way out of her arms and shook my head. "I'll never understand how your hot ass never got caught."

"Never got caught doing what?" Larry crept between us.

Shawnnie brushed against her husband. "What we did this morning," she whispered.

Larry turned red. "Why are y'all over here talking about that?" He glanced over to our girls waving at a pack of jocks flirting with them at the end of the hall. "Marshall, what'd ya say you and me take the girls for a quick bite and show'em one mo' time how to change a tire while their mothers finish getting their room ready."

"I could go for a bite," I said.

"Marshall and I will be sure to bring you two spirited young ladies whatever you want back."

Shawnnie nudged my arm. "Sounds good to me." She lowered her head and looked up at me with stretched eyes. "Father daughter time does sound like a great idea, doesn't it J.C.?"

"Yeah. It does." I kissed Marshall. "You know what I like. Just don't come back empty handed."

The guys broke up the girls checking out the merchandise in their new residence. Once they were out of earshot, I asked Shawnnie, "What are you up to?"

"You and I are going to set up their room, then go on a tour of this place. I wanna relive my old college days and see if I still got it."

"Didn't you get laid this morning? And no offense, but none of these young boys are looking at the likes of you and me when they are surrounded by girls who don't have to wear a bra yet."

Shawnnie spun around. "Speak for yourself."

We strolled a quarter of the campus, reading the history of the brick buildings glued by stone and cement in wall plaques. The Quad was deader than an unpopular kid's birthday party, and the soccer practice field was the scene of a break-up by two rude chil-dren yelling at us for privacy.

Shawnnie and I laughed all the way back to the dorm where the lobby had more action than the campus, and the top floor blasted music you could feel thump in the elevator.

"You thinking what I'm thinking?" Shawnnie raised her brows.

"I am not crashing my daughter's first college party. She'll kill me if word gets out." I stepped onto the third floor and pulled Shawnnie out of the elevator. "And you're not embarrassing Alex either."

"Sorry. Didn't mean to get in your way," said a voice as I flung Shawnnie into the hallway.

Chills froze on my back. My nipples recognized that deep, raspy voice before my brain processed its accent and regional diction. The hair on my arms prickled as I looked into his eyes. Those damn eyes. And those fucking lips.

We stared at each other in silence.

"Dad?" A younger version of him called while holding the elevator door open, making me rethink what I said about time travel.

"Yeah," he answered him while gazing deep into my eyes.

"Can we go?"

"Here." He tossed him the keys. "Pull the car around. I'll be down in a few minutes."

The boy let the elevator doors close.

Shawnnie villainously chuckled through a smirk. "I remember you, pretty boy." She looked at me. "I guess what they say is true. The tongue is a powerful thing."

"Shawnnie, here's the key to the room." I raised my arm. "I'll be in in a minute."

"No thanks. I'll be upstairs getting lit with the kids. Call me whenever, whatever this is going on right here, is done." She hopped on the elevator cackling.

The side of his mouth curved. "My God. You look the same."

"You don't have to flatter me. Time and age have hit us both." I pointed to the wrinkles on the sides of his eyes.

"Well it's been better to you than it has been to me. Come here." He swooped in for a hug.

'You're still as handsome as ever, but I wouldn't dare tell you that.'

"Thank you." I curved out of his arms.

He took a deep breath. "If this were back in the day, we'd be kissing by now."

I stared at the pudginess of his waist. "I see you had that pizza party without me."

He grinned and rubbed his stomach. "I could skip a few meals."

'Is he waiting for a compliment? Sure he is. He's testing me.'

I hummed as I snickered. "Nothing wrong with being fed well." A nervous laugh curled a smile on my face. "They say it means you're happy."

He smiled back at me, looked down at my hand, then back into my eyes. "I don't know about that, but I know what would make me the happiest man in the world."

An awkward silence snuck between us.

"So is he your only one?"

He stuttered. "Oh, my, my boy. Naw. I got two more knuckleheads behind him. How about you?"

"One girl."

His eyes shifted and his mouth twisted.

"You can stop doing the math. She's not yours."

"She should have been. I was trying for one that last time we…"

"I knew exactly what you were doing."

He licked his lips. "If only you knew how bad I want to relive that night right now."

I held up my hand. "Not gonna happen."

He sighed. "I looked for you, ya know."

"What on earth for?"

"I hated myself for the way things ended. I thought you would have calmed down after a couple of weeks, but you changed your number again, your mother told me to piss off, and Spencer said he didn't want to get involved."

I sucked my teeth. "Yeah. Not as long as you were giving him those tickets."

"Right. It's all he cared about." Cade's demeanor turned serious. "I kept giving him tickets hoping you would show up with him one day. I never got over you."

"Let's not go down Memory Lane."

"I say we do. What I knew then, I still know now."

"And what's that?"

"Losing you was the biggest mistake of my life."

I blushed. "Well, that's all in the past. Things worked out for the best, so getting you out of my system wasn't a mistake."

"Did you— get me out of your system?"

I scowled. "What did you think? I was sitting somewhere in a corner for nearly twenty years pining after you? Get over yourself, Cade."

"I didn't mean it like that."

"Yeah you did. Because you knew how much I loved you, yet you treated me like one of your trick plays. *Juke.*" I scoffed. "That name is fitting."

"J.C., I never stopped loving you." His intoxicating eyes glistened in the light as he stepped in closer to me.

I shuddered, recognizing the enchantment of those words stirring something in me. He still had it. The charisma. The delivery. The good looks. And the fucking audacity.

My heart rate increased as the lies he spieled hardened my nipples. I stepped backward, broke our gaze, and smiled before I sighed.

"After all these years, you still think that was love? You never loved me. I realized that once I met my husband."

"What I did to you was wrong. I was selfish."

"And misleading," I added.

"That, too. But I loved the hell out of you, and you know it."

"It was something. I'm not sure what though."

"So you didn't love me?"

"That's irrelevant now, don't you think?"

He stepped into my space again and cornered me on the wall. "This moment says otherwise. There's a reason for everything. A reason we met. And a reason fate keeps bringing us together."

Nervously, I looked around for witnesses. In the blink of an eye, Cade stood inches away from my face. A hint of fresh lavender and mint stormed my nose and my senses came alive. His eyes began working its magic, hypnotizing me of illicit actions and past coital encounters.

My pussy throbbed as I slid out of the danger zone. "Look at us. Two decades later at our children's school talking about something that doesn't matter anymore. Allow me to reset this conversation. How have you been?"

His fingers tickled mine.

I pushed them away. "Cade, I asked you a question. How's life been treating you?"

"Pretty good. Great right now that I'm finally getting my wish to see you again. I didn't think this day would ever come. What would happen if I kissed you right now?"

Desire burned with intensity between my legs. "I won't let you do that."

I swallowed hard and walked towards the girl's room. Cade pressed on my heels calling me, "Sweetness." I sped up my pace, telling myself to be smart and not allow his charm, and our history, put me in a position to be manhandled against the wall in my daughter's room for a five minute quickie.

The devil stood on my shoulder and placed that image in my mind, and I thought I could be the one to actually revisit the good ole days, instead of my sister upstairs reliving her youth at a frat party.

I could feel him one more time, and no one would know. Then, I remembered in doing so, I'd be letting him win, when I was the one who walked away from him twenty years ago.

He stood behind me as I fumbled, placing the key in the lock. "Do I make you that nervous?"

I held my breath and stopped scrambling with the lock.

"Jaya Marcel. The woman I have looked for, for the past twenty years, hoping to get a chance to right my wrong. The woman I have carried a torch for, for two decades. And here you are. Still gorgeous. Still sexy. Still riling me up without even trying. Please tell me I can taste your sweet lips, Sweetness?"

I turned around. "Cade, you've always had a way with words, but if I were to say yes, I'd be the stupidest fucking woman on the planet."

His face fell.

"Only an idiot would risk losing the man of her dreams for the man who once danced in them just to give me nightmares. I would look in the mirror and hate myself for allowing you to swindle me with meaningless words, and the man I love now would have every reason to hate me and drop me like gravity." I chuckled. "A kiss from the likes of you is not worth me losing him. And, I don't want it."

Cade backed away.

"But, I do hope your son has an amazing year." I unlocked the room door. "What's his name?"

"CJ, my junior."

"As he should be. He looks just like you. I'll be sure to tell my girls to make sure they stay away from him. Lovely seeing you again."

I rushed inside the girl's room and leaned my back against the door. Moments later, the handle jiggled and I gasped.

"J.C., open up." Shawnnie's voice traveled through the door.

I held my chest. "Thank God it's you."

"I came to brag that I've still got it going on, and to make sure your ass wasn't spread in that good looking devil's face. Age didn't hurt him, and he was looking at you like he still wanted a piece."

I raised my brows. "Let's pretend we never saw him."

"That's probably for the best."

"But how can we make sure our girls stay away from his boy?"

"Shit, I saw that boy. If we say anything, we'll be driving them straight into his lap."

"Umph. Let us pray."

It was time to say good-bye and my chest crushed in pieces letting go of my daughter. Leaving her at a building filled with strangers and curiosity felt like I was releasing her into the wild and abandoning my duty as her mother.

Danielle and Alexandria walked us down to the lobby. Marshall was forced to pry Dani from my arms, and led me out of the hall with a face full of tears running down my face.

He held my hand as we caught up with Shawnnie and Larry waiting for us on the steps past the courtyard.

"I'll take the first shift back," said Larry.

Marshall squeezed me with one arm as he passed the keys to him. "Thanks man, 'cause this one is a mess."

"Good evening," Cade said as he walked past us with his son.

"What's up?" Larry tapped Marshall's shoulder. "Ain't that the running back?"

Shawnnie and I glared at each other.

Marshall nodded. "I think so."

Cade turned around.

"Juke, right?" Larry asked.

Cade double backed and shook Larry's hand. "Nice to meet you." He looked Marshall up and down. "You played ball didn't you?" He extended his hand.

Marshall gave him a pound. "Center Field for a few years in B-More."

"Yeah. Yeah. I thought you looked familiar. My boy is following my footsteps down here. How about you?"

"Nah. My daughter isn't into sports. I got an academic scholar on my hands."

Shawnnie pulled me away. "Over and done with my ass. How is it that Marshall doesn't know about you and him?" she whispered through gritted teeth.

"Good thing about being kept a secret is no one knew about me when he was in the spotlight. Marshall thinks I was tagging along with Spencer and Porsha when we met."

Shawnnie exhaled sharply. "Let's break this shit up right now."

"Please, do something."

"Excuse me honey." Shawnnie pulled on her husband. "We need to get on the road." Shawnnie smiled at Cade. "Nice meeting you."

"Yeah, I gotta finish getting my boy settled in myself. Nice to meet you guys as well." He glazed me over with a cheap grin.

The crisis had been diverted, or so I thought. Larry unlocked the doors to the car we were driving back home when suddenly Marshall stopped in his tracks with a pensive look on his face.

"What is it?" I asked him.

He turned around. "I don't like how that Juke fella stared at you."

I lied. "I didn't notice."

"If it were back in the day, I would have knocked him on his ass."

"It's not too late." I joked. "Seeing you state your claim is kind of a turn on."

"Oh yeah. You like hearing me say you're mine, ey."

"I do. Say it again."

"Mine." He palmed my ass. "Think we can convince those two to grab a hotel and stay overnight."

I squeezed his arm. "And we could surprise the girls in the morning."

"Never mind. Let's get you home. It's been years since I've had you on the kitchen counter."

Marshall opened my door. I looked back at the dorms one more time, then settled in the car.

Shawnnie pinched my leg. "They're going to do just fine," she said, covertly pointing to the steps before Marshall hopped in on his side.

Cade stood at the bottom of the steps watching us from a shaded corner below the lamppost. His once enchanting, honey colored eyes met with mine from a distance, failing to work their magic.

I grinned to myself that the spell he once casted on me was no more, and he was able to see how I ended up better off, wiser, and happy without him.

He played and lost. I moved on and won.

As I said before, there are love stories where two people meet by chance and fall in love until the end of time. Ours was filled with passion linked by destiny on the high tide of lust floating in the wind, bringing about an illicit affair that taught me the truth about love, and a lesson about life. That passion and destiny was our ballad. And this the end of our reprise, for I will remember our time together as a mere verse in my song.

Afterword

To the woman whose husband
I fell in love with.
If I had known you existed,
this story would have never taken place.
At least not with me.

~J.C.

REVIEWS ENCOURAGE VORACIOUS INTEREST EVERY WHERE TO SUPPORT

ME, THE AUTHOR

I GREATLY APPRECIATE IT

T.K. RICHARDS is a multi-genre author of women's fiction and romance, featuring popular novels and novellas in Black Romance, Interracial/Multicultural Romance, Paranormal Romance, and YA Fiction. You can find her serialized fiction work on the Kindle Vella app. A graduate of Limestone University, T.K. has honors in Expository Writing, and was also the Poet Laureate of her graduating class. When she is not writing, she is immersed in the world of tennis, and binge watching movies—mostly comedy as she loves to laugh.

For more information about **T.K. Richards**, visit her website at www.tkrichards.com or subscribe to her newsletter at: https://tkrichardsnewsletter.ck.page

You can follow T.K. RICHARDS on the platforms listed below to interact with her personally:

facebook.com/Tkrichards

twitter.com/tkrichards1

instagram.com/t.k.richards

pinterest.com/TKWrites

tiktok.com/@tkrwrites

youtube.com/tkrichards

goodreads.com/T.k.richards

bookbub.com/authors/t-k-richards

amazon.com/author/Tkrichards

Acknowledgments

To R.B. (your private arse☺) I can never repay you for the many times you've provided, guided, and saved me. Thank you for always coming through for me in a clutch.

To my encouragement squad:

Racquel Henry
Kimani Lauren
Markeshia Kirksey
Ashley Coleman
Anita Nelson
Mia Lindler
Sarah Ushurhe
Carolyn Taylor

Thank you for your listening ears, your words, and your support.

Music & Books

To the readers who love soundtracks with their books, all song titles are by one of my favorite artists. The amazing Sade. Find me on Spotify to enjoy this curated playlist.

BY T.K. RICHARDS

  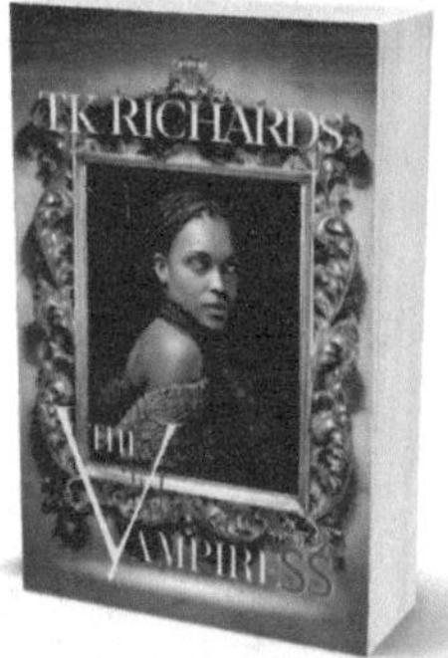